The **HOUSE** that went **DOWN** with the **SHIP**

Books by David Healey

Novels
Sharpshooter
Rebel Fever
Rebel Train
Winter Sniper
Time Reich
First Voyage: The Sea Lord Chronicles
The House That Went Down With The Ship

Nonfiction
1812: Rediscovering Chesapeake Bay's
Forgotten War
Delmarva Legends & Lore
Great Storms of the Chesapeake

The HOUSE that went DOWN with the SHIP

A Delmarva Renovators Mystery

DAVID HEALEY

BellaRosaBooks

BellaRosaBooks

The House That Went Down With The Ship
ISBN 978-1-62268-028-3

First Edition June 2013

Library of Congress Control Number: 2013942415

Also available in e-book form: ISBN 978-1-62268-029-0

Cover illustration by Nick Deligaris www.deligaris.com

BellaRosaBooks and logo are trademarks of Bella Rosa Books.

10   9   8   7   6   5   4   3   2   1

Acknowledgements

Like an old house, a book takes a lot of people to get everything just right. Initial chapters of this story got their first rehabbing at the Stonecoast MFA pop fiction workshop. Professional renovator and mystery fan Rebecca Mann made several valuable suggestions. Sharp-eyed editor Rod Hunter sanded out the rough patches. And finally, the author's family put up with the general dust and noise that any writing project generates, particularly when the story is loosely based on their own 1913 foursquare house.

The HOUSE that went DOWN with the SHIP

"A man builds a fine house; and now he has a master, and a task for life: he is to furnish, watch, show it, and keep it in repair, the rest of his days."
—Ralph Waldo Emerson

CHAPTER 1

Later that morning, after we found the body, I realized that the sight of such a long-dead person didn't bother me all that much. Working on an old house, you have to be prepared for just about anything. Sparking wires. Bats. Leaky plumbing. Bodies. And did I mention the flying tools?

"Heads up!"

I barely had time to shout a warning before Mac's hammer sailed through the dining room to punch a hole in the plaster wall. A fine powder drifted up and horsehair bristles sprouted from the edges of the hole. I sighed. One more job for the renovation list.

"Son of a moth-eaten whore!" Mac waved the thumb he had smashed moments before with the offending hammer. "That's the second time today."

"Maybe you ought to wear your glasses," I suggested, motioning at our cameraman, Iggy, to take a break.

"What kind of TV show carpenter wears glasses?" demanded Mac, who was now holding his throbbing thumb and doing a kind of jig across the dusty floor. The house shook under his weight.

"The kind who doesn't whack his thumb," I said.

Robert "Mac" MacDonough was six foot four, built square and solid as a refrigerator, and there are firecrackers with longer fuses. When Mac gets mad, I've seen him pick up cinder blocks and hurl them like horseshoes.

Once, I watched Mac toss three guys out a window at a construction job when they tried to pull a fast one with some shoddy work—lucky for them we were only on the first floor. Working with Mac, I had learned better than to provoke him, and I was proud to say he hadn't flung me out any windows yet.

I'd known Mac for twenty years, ever since we'd been thrown together as college roommates. In fact, it was Mac who had given me the nickname when he learned that my last name—Martell—meant "Hammer" in French. Back then, the nickname had more to do with how many beers I could chug, but I had developed new skills in the intervening decades. Mac and I even got our introduction to home improvement together, working for contractors every summer to earn our beer money. I had gone on to a career in magazine editing and Mac had become a builder. Both of our careers had evaporated in the Great Recession, and now we were back together, producing our own on-line home improvement show based on the Delmarva Peninsula, that long spit of land between the Chesapeake and Delaware bays that was a world unto itself.

Mac was more than a little nearsighted, but I couldn't get him to wear his glasses while we were filming. Maybe it was simple vanity or maybe, like me, he didn't want to admit that we weren't as young as we used to be. One of these days he was going to cut off something important, and then he'd be sorry. Depending on what he was holding at the time, we all might be.

Mac was much better at acts of brute strength than he was at carpentry. He served as our licensed contractor. He was good at threatening and cajoling lazy subcontractors into getting the job done right. He was also currently the acting star of our show, *Delmarva Renovators*. Maybe you've seen the Web cast? Our real star had disappeared in the middle of our first big rehabbing project. She hadn't quit—it wasn't like Jenny Cooper to quit anything—but she had made some vague excuses about "some business to take care of" and said that she needed some time off. It was no small coincidence that her departure had come shortly after a late-night editing session had wound up with Jenny in my bed. So far, nobody else knew about our little tryst, and I was trying hard to keep it that way.

"Okay, when the crew comes back, I want to explain exactly what you're doing," I said.

"What am I doing?"

"Anything but whacking your thumb. For starters, see if you can pry off some of that molding. We want to save as much of the original woodwork as we can."

The molding around the doors and windows was more than five inches wide, with lovely rosettes in all the corners. Replicating it would cost us time and money, and we were already over budget. It had to come off so we could access the antique pocket doors. There was no way to do the work short of taking down the wall, which was going to be a messy and time-consuming job that threatened to put us even further behind schedule, short-handed as we were.

Our project was a waterfront four-square house in the historic district of the small town of Chesapeake City on Maryland's Eastern Shore. The house had more problems than a stray cat has fleas, but it was also a gem deep down, which made it perfect for our inaugural show.

Built in 1913, the house had been home to six generations of the Cosden family before being sold to a couple who had made a bundle running a service franchise on the Western Shore—which was how local people referred to anything on the other side of Chesapeake Bay, as if it were a slightly foreign country, like Canada. A lot of Cosdens still lived in Chesapeake City, and it rubbed them the wrong way that the home of their patriarch, Captain Ezra Cosden, had gone to outsiders from the D.C. suburbs. Some of the extended family had even taken to hanging around and watching the progress on the house with the same mournful expressions on their faces that Confederate veterans must have worn for the surrender at Appomattox. You would have thought the Cosdens would be grateful we were preserving their family home, but they seemed more concerned that some of the family history was going to be tossed into the industrial-sized Dumpster out front on Third Street.

Amazingly, the house had gone nearly untouched for most of its long history. There was indoor plumbing, electric and a furnace, but that was almost the only concession to modern conveniences. Not that any of those systems were in great shape. The plumbing consisted of leaky copper tubing and there wasn't so much as a single vent pipe. The electrical system was a spaghetti bowl of modern wiring cobbled to downright scary knob and tube, an early form of wiring that resembled an electric fence inside the walls and ceilings. It was a wonder the house hadn't burned down by now. The furnace, converted from a coal-burner, was the size of a locomotive and slathered in asbestos. Every time that behemoth clicked on, I was sure that a small oil well somewhere in the world ran dry.

No air conditioning, no insulation. Definitely no new roof in the last four decades. On windy days, bits of crumbling slate shingles rained down on the lawn. Termites. A colony of bats lived in the attic. Evicting them had made for great video, although some of the leathery winged residents stubbornly refused to leave.

Over the years, the Cosdens had attempted a few home improvements, all of which we were having to undo. Every wall was blanketed in multiple layers of old-fashioned wallpaper. Nearly every ceiling had been covered with asbestos tiles. The reason for that became clear when we pulled away the tiles to discover that the plaster ceilings were sagging away from the lath beneath. In the single bathroom upstairs, some trendy Cosden in the 1970s had stuck down adhesive-backed squares of lime-green shag carpeting around the original claw foot tub. All of it—the wallpaper, the ceiling tiles, the sagging plaster, the shag—had to go.

The good news was that under those cosmetic nightmares,

the house was solid and filled with fine details. Truly, it was a lovely old home. Two sets of pocket doors with the original brass hardware slid out to enclose what had been the living room. The cast iron radiators featured intricate scroll work that our interior designer, Marsha LaRue, planned to highlight with a fine brush so that each radiator was like a work of art. The staircase still had its original coat of shellac, having been spared the paintbrush. The crowning feature of the house was a widow's walk where in decades past the Cosdens could literally watch for their father's ship to come in. And the view of the Chesapeake and Delaware Canal was to die for.

Four-squares were the ranch houses of the early 1900s, a popular and economical building style for the time, though Captain Cosden's was built on a grander scale than most. They took their name from their design—almost always square, sometimes rectangular on a small lot (like the Cosden House). The yard was small, but Captain Cosden had been a Chesapeake Bay captain, not a gardener. Four-squares were so named because they had four rooms downstairs—foyer, living room, dining room, kitchen. Most had three or four bedrooms upstairs. Our project house had three, not counting the bath that was big as the smaller bedroom, plus a large walk-up attic that functioned as an unfinished third floor. Completing the attic— and evicting the bats for good—was part of our plan. Finally, like all other four-squares, the Cosden House had a hip roof, but with a leaky dormer in each side. Add them to the renovation list. It was the job of *Delmarva Renovators* to update the Cosden House for the twenty-first century while keeping the best of the early twentieth, all for the entertainment and edification of our on-line viewers.

Trouble was, we were running out of time. The new owners were planning a big housewarming party in late June during the town's annual Canal Day street festival. We'd had six months to get the job done and we were already deep into the fifth. They were footing the bill for the renovation work, but we were perilously close to being over our budget of two hundred thousand dollars. The money went toward materials and sub-contractors. The homeowners were essentially getting our labor for free. Our only paycheck came from the revenue provided by *Delmarva Renovators*. And that was pretty skimpy so far.

According to our contract, the homeowners weren't obligated to give us a single nickel—or a single day—beyond what we had agreed upon. Short of a miracle—and the reappearance of our charismatic host and master carpenter—it was going to be hard to come in within budget and on schedule. People watched home improvement shows partly because the race-against-time created drama and suspense. Our show was never going to get off the ground if our first full-house project didn't have a happy ending.

Iggy came back with a tall cup of coffee and our gofer, Kat, in tow. They made an interesting study in contrasts. Kat was maybe nineteen and had what appeared to be the contents of half a jewelry store glittering from her ears, eyebrows, nose and lips—and God knows where else. Tall and skinny, Iggy was vague about his age, but he looked somewhere between thirty and fifty, judging from the strands of gray mixed with the long black hair of his ponytail. He wore black boots, black jeans, a black silk shirt and oversized, wrap-around eyeglasses like Bono. But Iggy was no poseur. He was good with a camera and fearless, willing to crawl into the darkest crawl space or balance on a windy rooftop. Sometimes, I thought Iggy might follow the action into hell itself if need be.

He gave his ponytail a shake, then took a big swig of coffee. I used to think of myself as a caffeine junkie until I met Iggy. His Adam's apple bobbed up and down as he swallowed—make that gulped—the coffee. "So, what are we doing?"

"Trim molding," I said. "Mac is going to show us how to salvage it."

"Okay." Iggy reached for his camera. He had another camera set up nearby on a tripod so that he could cut back and forth between angles. Kat rigged up one of the umbrella lights. Mac shook out his sore thumb one last time. Then he got down on one knee next to the wall with the pocket door. He was working in the corner where the dining room wall concealing the pocket door met the structural interior dining room wall at a right angle.

"Tell us some of the history behind the wood, Mac," I prompted. "The saw mill, remember?"

He nodded and our gofer handed him a molding bar and a hammer. "Hit yourself with that again and we're going to make you sit in the truck the rest of the day," she warned.

"I'd like to see you try and make me, girlie girl."

"Happy thoughts, everybody," I said. "Go."

Mac scowled at the camera. "What we're going to do now is—very carefully—pry off some of this molding so that we can reuse it once we're finished working on the new wall." He held up what looked like a smaller, more elegant version of a crow bar and Iggy zoomed in on it. "We'll be using this tool here, which is commonly called a pry bar. Look at the shape of it—the flat end here slides under trim molding to pull it away from the wall with as little damage as possible. It's for prying with a light touch." He pointed to the other end. "For those stubborn nails, there's also a notched tip to pull them out."

Mac went on: "Now, why bother with the molding? First off, you're not going to find a hardware store that carries anything like this. Close, but it won't have the width we need. So we want to save it. It's in pretty good shape. Second, this molding has some historical value because, like all the lumber in the house, it was actually produced at a saw mill that once stood about a hundred yards behind the house. Years ago, they used to float logs from Pennsylvania down the Susquehanna River into the Chesapeake Bay, then on to the canal, which is why the saw mill was located on the waterfront. That saw mill disappeared when the U.S. Army Corps of Engineers widened the canal in the 1920s, so it's not like we can go back in time and get more wood."

I nodded encouragement. He was doing fine. Mac worked the molding bar under the trim and was tugging to loosen the nails that held it to the door framing. Iggy zoomed in with his hand-held camera. One by one, the nails popped free, some of them sounding loud as gun shots.

The last couple of nails were stubborn. A bit more finesse might have done the trick, but this was Mac we were talking about. The big veins on the side of his neck stood out like cables as he strained to make the nails release their grip.

"Just a little more," he said for benefit of the camera.

The molding gave way with a rending shriek. The piece of trim seemed to explode off the wall. Mac went flying backward, fending off wood and plaster with a big forearm. His full weight hit the dining room wall behind him. An ominous cracking sound followed. He threw up his hands to protect his head as a large section of sand plaster wall collapsed.

"Mac!" I cried, but I quickly saw that the plaster wasn't heavy enough to do any real damage and that he wasn't hurt. My concern soon changed to annoyance that Mac's clumsiness had just created another major job for us when we were already behind schedule. Having both walls come down at once was definitely not part of the script. Iggy bent over the camera, protecting it as best he could while trying to shoot despite the swirling dust. There was nothing so messy on a rehab job as demolished plaster. It coated everything with a powder fine as talcum. Silently, I said a prayer of thanks that we hadn't yet refinished any of the floors in the house or even put on a coat of paint.

Choking and coughing, Mac sat on the floor, covered in crumbled sand plaster. He looked like he'd been rolled in flour. He still clutched the molding bar. The salvaged trim molding lay across his knees. When the lath and plaster gave way, a bundle of rags about half as big as Mac had come tumbling out of the wall. It now lay on the floor beside him.

"What's that?" Iggy said.

We all took a step closer. As the swirling cloud of debris cleared, the bundle began to take on shape. Mac swept some crumbled plaster off the rags and it became clear that the rags were, in fact, a very dusty suit.

And at the top of the suit was a mummified face.

Like a huge dried apple with deep-set eyes, the face stared back at us. If I hadn't known better, I would have sworn the corpse had an angry expression. The lips had shrunken to reveal teeth the color of old ivory, caught in an eternal scowl that somehow looked familiar. Wisps of brown hair fell down over the mummy's face.

That was the moment that our decorator chose to walk in. Marsha LaRue took one look at the grinning corpse on the floor, its head nearly in Mac's lap, and let out a scream that rattled the old windows in their frames.

Iggy's camera was rolling the whole time. "Ladies and gentlemen," he said. "I'd call that a wrap."

CHAPTER 2

One hour later, we were still waiting for the police to show up. Not that there was any hurry. All indications were that the body in the wall had been dead for a long, long time, maybe even since the house was built. Hardly a lights-and-sirens situation. Meanwhile, the crew and cast of *Delmarva Renovators* stood around trying to figure out how and why a body had come to be in the wall.

I glanced at my watch, feeling a stab of guilt that I could even think about our work schedule under the circumstances. But in the renovation world, time really was money. Some days I went around grumbling like John Wayne in *The Cowboys*, "We're burning daylight, people."

So I was finding it hard to summon much sympathy for the dried-up body that had tumbled out of the wall and brought everything to a standstill. At the same time, like everyone else, I was plenty curious. And I was beginning to have this feeling that finding a body in our project house wasn't such a bad thing at all. Bodies make good stories; good stories make good content; good content meant lots of visitors to our website. It was just the boost our fledgling online show needed. If I'd felt a stab of guilt at being unhappy over the waste of time, the thought of benefiting from a dead man plunged the knife in the rest of the way.

But first things first. Who was this guy and how did he

come to be walled up inside the Cosden House?

I looked around at the bare studs, the wires poking from the ceiling, the floor strewn with chunks of broken plaster. If the police didn't arrive soon, I was at least going to have everyone get to work sweeping up so that they would be ready to start shooting again first thing in the morning. That stab of guilt was quickly fading to something like a twinge or a pinch.

Mac was inspecting the remains. "It's definitely a man," he said.

"How can you tell?" I asked.

He gave me a look. "One big clue is that he's not wearing a dress."

"Good point."

"I don't see any obvious signs of trauma. But short of the medical examiner taking a look, it's hard to say what's under the dust and cobwebs."

"What would you know about it?" Marsha snapped. I suspected that Marsha was embarrassed that she had lost control of herself and ripped out such a scream at seeing the body. Consequently, she had returned to her business-like self.

"Don't forget that I used to be a cop," said Mac. "For two years, down in Baltimore."

Marsha sniffed. "Writing parking tickets does not make one a homicide investigator."

Mac swatted at his arms, raising clouds of plaster dust. "Who said anything about homicide? At this point it's just a body that was in the wall."

"What, you think somebody put it there by accident?" she scoffed.

I was always forgetting Mac's career as a cop. He quit after having to hold back a mother whose four-year-old was the innocent victim of a drive-by shooting. He had stood there, wrapping the mother in a bear hug, watching as they zipped her child into a body bag.

"It was the saddest damn thing I ever saw, Hammer," he told me later. "I knew right then that if I stayed on, my heart was either going to break or it was going to shrink."

Mac took a step closer to the mummified remains. Chunks of plaster crunched under his boots. "Definitely a man," he said. "And get a load of those clothes."

We did, creeping forward as a group. Only Iggy and Kat hung back, filming the rest of us. Closer up, I could see what Mac meant.

"Early twentieth century or maybe late nineteenth," Marsha remarked, adding her more expert opinion. She lived and breathed antiques and fabrics so I trusted her observation regarding the dead man's clothes.

It was hard to see past the dust. But as I looked closer, I noticed that the shirt itself was collarless, the kind you saw workmen wearing in old-time photographs. It was his shoes that jumped out at me. They were cut high like work boots and—even accounting for the fact that they might be dry-rotted—it looked as if they had seen better days.

"He was a working man," Mac said. "Maybe he died on the job and they plastered right over him. Poor bastard. Here, let's look in his pockets."

"Shouldn't we wait for the police?" Kat said. "We don't want to mess anything up." She sounded nervous. I had to wonder if maybe the kid was exhibiting more sense than the so-called mature adults in the room.

"I'd say this crime scene is beyond disturbing," Mac pointed out. "We've pretty much torn down the walls all around him. The question is, did he go into the wall alive or dead?"

Beside me, I felt Marsha shiver. "Ooh, it's like that Edgar Allan Poe story, *The Cask of Amontillado*, where he walls up his enemy in the catacombs."

"If somebody tried to put me in a wall, I'd fight back plenty hard," Mac said. He took a cat's paw—a foot-long hooked tool used for digging out nails—off a windowsill and poked at the corpse. "No rope on his hands or feet. I'd say he was dead or maybe unconscious when he went behind the wall."

"In *The Cask of Amontillado* he chains his victim inside a wine cellar closes up the wall with bricks," I said, struggling to recall the short story from high school English class. "This wall was just sand plaster and lath. You could break out of that. I'd say he was already dead."

"Good and dead," Mac agreed. "Somebody stuck him in here and walled him up."

"Who is he?" Marsha asked.

"That's the million dollar question, isn't it?" Mac said.

The thought that we had been working for months in the company of human remains was spooky. If Mac hadn't knocked down the wall, the body might have gone undiscovered for as long as the house stood.

It was clear that the body had been sealed inside the wall rather hastily. In an old house like this, the studs were first covered with wood lath that was about three-eighths of an inch thick and an inch wide. Normally, the lath was nailed on so that there was just a small gap between the strips. The plaster—a mixture of sand, plaster dust and horsehair, mixed on the job (possibly with water from the canal)—was then smoothed over the lath, so that it oozed between the gaps. Once the plaster dried, the lath bonded it securely to the walls.

Here, though, the lath strips had been widely spaced. That was why the entire wall—plaster, lath and all—had given way so easily when Mac's weight fell against it. What became clear, too, was that the body had been hidden behind a false wall, rather than one planned as part of the initial construction. The main clue to this fact was that the pine flooring behind the wall matched the dining room floor. To the left of the fireplace in the middle of the dining room wall there should have been an alcove maybe eighteen inches deep and five feet wide. The false wall had been built right across it, creating a hidden crypt. Some thought had been given to hiding this body.

Mac took another step toward the corpse and starting hooking the cat's paw inside the pockets. Of the many ways that a cat's paw could be used, most of which involved prying things apart and hooking out stubborn nails, I was pretty sure this was a first. But it was not an ideal tool. Mac reached down and probed the pockets with his fingers. Iggy still had the camera going.

"What are you doing?" Marsha asked, sounding aghast.

"Trying to figure out who this poor bugger was," Mac explained, flipping open the suit coat to go through the inside pockets. "Maybe there's a wallet or something."

"You should let the police do that," Kat said.

But there was no stopping Mac. "At this point I'd say the body falls into the category of old house relic. There aren't going to be any clues but the obvious ones, like a dagger in his back."

The pockets didn't reveal a thing, even after Mac had turned them inside out. Not a coin, not a scrap of paper. The man in the wall wasn't making it easy on us.

"Somebody toss me a pair of gloves," Mac said.

"Rubber or leather?" Iggy asked.

"If he tells the corpse to turn its head and cough, I'm leaving," I said. "Seriously, Mac, don't you think you ought to let that thing alone?"

Mac slipped on a pair of gloves and brushed at the corpse's leathery left hand, which was clenched into a fist. "There might be something in his hand," he said. "If I can just straighten out the fingers—"

With a dry snap, the ring finger broke off in Mac's grip. The mummified hand was empty.

"I think I'm going to be sick," Marsha said. "Can't you be more careful?"

Mac didn't have a chance to answer before someone called "Hello?" through the open front door. Mac was still standing over the body, holding the corpse's finger like a desiccated chicken wing, when a sheriff's deputy walked in.

To the deputy's credit, she didn't say anything right away, but just kind of absorbed the situation. I could only imagine what she thought. There was Iggy, tall and garbed in black; Kat glittering with body piercings; Marsha with a purple scarf draped theatrically around her ebony neck; me standing there about to hand Mac a pair of gloves and then Mac himself crouched over the corpse like a predatory bear. If an artist had chosen to capture the scene on canvas he could have called the painting "Still Life at the Asylum."

When the deputy finally spoke she lingered over each word as if she was afraid we might have trouble understanding. I suppose we did look like a roomful of idiots.

"What . . . in . . . hell . . . is going on here?"

The police car in front of our project house drew a crowd. By the time two more police cars showed up, and then the Maryland State Police Crime Scene Unit, the street was full of curious town residents. As the police did their job, I stepped out on the front porch to talk with some of our neighbors. There was Carl Batzer, who ran the Bohemia Café, and Maggie Delpino, who had an antiques shop called The Magpie. Iver Jones had an antiques shop and Pete Morrison was a painter who specialized in Chesapeake Bay historical scenes.

Several of the faces in the crowd belonged to Cosdens. You could pick them out because they all had a kind of family scowl that only grew more pronounced with age. It was the same fierce expression worn by Captain Ezra Cosden in a photograph that hung at the town museum. I saw old Edith Cosden, tall and lean as a whip, standing next to her daughter, Sarah. It had been Edith who sold the house out of the family when the upkeep and repairs got to be too much. She and Sarah now lived in an apartment in town above one of the shops.

There were a couple of male members of the clan present as well, snowy-haired Francis Cosden and his nephew, Rory Cosden. Early on, Rory had been particularly interested in our project. He had come around the house many times but no matter how friendly I was, he always greeted me with that Cosden scowl. Big and hulking, Rory couldn't have been more than twenty-eight or so—a young man from my point of view—but he hoarded his smiles as if they were gold.

The truth was that I had tried to reach out to the Cosdens in hopes that they would be as excited about seeing their old family home restored as I was, but they were a sour bunch whose family fortunes had crested decades ago when Captain Cosden was the town's leading citizen. And yet the Cosdens remained a force to be reckoned with because they were the thread that ran through the fabric of town life: a Cosden sat on the town council, another worked at the post office, several were members of the fire company and a Cosden ran the only gas station and garage for ten miles around. The people who had the studios and shops and restaurants were all newcomers, but old town families like the Cosdens were the ones who kept their cars running and put out the fires.

"Tom, what's going on?" Pete asked. He must have come right from the studio because his shirt was flecked with paint. "We heard you found a body in there."

"Somebody from about eighty years ago," I said. "He was inside a wall."

Quickly, I summed up the details for Pete and the others, who pressed closer to the porch—all except the Cosdens, who kept their distance. Everyone was asking me questions at once. I was answering them as best I could when a witchy, creaking voice rose above the noise and made us all look to the sidewalk, where Edith Cosden stood grim-faced.

"No good will come of it," she said, her voice rasping like a rusty hinge. "Some things are better off forgotten. I'm telling you that this house is cursed!"

We all just stared until Maggie finally spoke up and asked, "Edith, what in the world are you talking about?"

"I'm telling you they should have let well enough alone with this house," she said. "Now they've gone and let the curse out like a pack of wild dogs. That's not going to be the only body, I can tell you."

"Mother," the younger Cosden woman said, taking Edith by the elbow. "You've said enough."

"I'm just warning them," Edith said.

But she let herself be led away.

"She sounds like a character in a B horror movie," Maggie whispered beside me.

Still scowling, Francis and Rory Cosden gave the house a final look, then followed Edith and her daughter. Rory looked back over his shoulder once and caught my eye. It was a cold look, but I didn't know what he meant by it. Maybe another warning? I wondered what his problem was, considering that in Rory's case I had made an effort to cross the great Cosden divide. I had even hired him to do some of the work around the house, although he hadn't shown up much lately.

"Oh boy," Maggie said, watching them go. "Things never get dull in a small town, do they?"

While I was still on the porch, a deputy came out and strung yellow crime scene tape across the front door. I had to walk around to the back door to get back in. There, I found the crew of *Delmarva Renovators* more or less confined to the shell of the kitchen. Iggy was in the middle of arguing with a deputy and he waved me over.

"Tom, he wants to confiscate our video of the corpse being discovered."

I turned to the deputy. "You can't do that!"

"It's evidence," he said, crossing his arms on his chest. "I'll get a court order if I need to, but if you make me go to all that trouble I promise you I'll shut down this whole project."

I looked at Iggy, not sure what to do. But he just shrugged, showing an uncharacteristic lack of concern, and handed over the memory card from his camera. I almost reached out to grab it. Right now, that video was our best chance of getting noticed on the Web.

The deputy slipped the card containing our video of the body's discovery into a pocket. It was a little like the feeling you might have experienced if you've ever watched a wedding ring swirling down the bathroom drain. "That was the right choice, fellas. I knew you'd see it my way."

Mac was looming in a corner of the kitchen, looking as sullen as I felt. The police had given him a good dressing down for going through the dead man's pockets, not to mention snapping off a finger. The cops had made it plain they were unhappy with all of us for our disruption of the body and the crime scene itself.

The deputy who had first arrived at the house came in. She cleared her throat and hooked her thumbs in her utility belt, just like a good ol' boy would have done. But she was far different from any of the other deputies who had descended on the Cosden House. This one was taller than most of the men, and in better shape. It was hard for anyone to look good in those dark blue pants with the gray stripe and blue uniform shirt, but she filled them out nicely. Her brown hair was done up in a business-like bun. She wore glasses with heavy black frames; behind the lenses, her eyes were robin's egg blue. I guessed she was in her early thirties.

"Which one of you is in charge here?" the deputy asked.

Since my crew was now all looking at me, I figured it must be unanimous. "That would be me, I guess."

"You don't sound so sure about that."

"Deputy, with the way things have been going around here I'm not sure I could tell you what day of the week it is. I'm Tom Martell."

"DFC Maureen Sullivan," she said, thrusting out a hand. Face to face, I was surprised to see that she was maybe an inch taller than me, which would have made her about six-one. Her grip was strong. She pumped my hand once and let go.

"First off, I need to see your building permit," DFC Sullivan said.

"Our building permit? It's posted right out front—"

I stopped myself when I saw the glimmer of mischief dancing in her big blue eyes. Still, I couldn't help but feel my temper start to slip. My sense of humor was caked in plaster dust. Annoyed now, I asked, "Have you caught the killer yet?"

She made a noise then that could best be described as a

guffaw. "Mr. Martell, it looks to me like that body's been in the wall since Calvin Coolidge was president. There's not going to be any killer to catch at this point."

"So are you still treating this like a homicide?"

"More like a biohazard," she said. "You shouldn't have touched that sucker—no telling what you might pick up. He might have died from Spanish flu or something."

"How long do you think this is going to hold us up?" I asked. "We've got a lot of work to do."

"It's nice to see your concern for the victim."

"You're the one who—"

"You should be good to go by tomorrow morning," DFC Sullivan said, eyes twinkling again at having gotten a rise out of me. She seemed to enjoy pushing my buttons. "I'll check with the crime scene boys, but I think they'll be done."

"That's some good news."

"I'll see what I can do to move them along," the deputy added. She hesitated, as if not quite sure if she should say something, then blurted out: "I've seen your show, you know."

"You have?" I was a little surprised. We weren't exactly a household name yet, though we had certainly caused a stir in Chesapeake City.

"I've got an old house myself," she said by way of explanation. "It's sort of a hodgepodge, but it started out as a log cabin around 1750 and kind of went from there."

"I'd love to see it sometime."

The deputy took out a business card and scribbled a number on the back. "Call me anytime. We'll set something up."

DFC Sullivan walked out, wiggling her hips a bit. It was the sort of walk that stopped just short of a sashay—or at least as much of a sashay as she could do wearing a deputy's uniform. She turned her head and gave me a hint of a smile as she went out.

As soon as she was gone, Mac came over and punched me on the arm so hard that I staggered. "You've still got the touch,

Hammer."

"Hey, what can I say? Must be my natural animal magnetism." I couldn't help thinking that Mac wouldn't have quite the same reaction if he'd known what happened between me and Jenny.

Mac arched his eyebrows and grinned. "Huh. I wonder if that's what your wife would call it?"

CHAPTER 3

I had called my boys and was updating our website around nine p.m. when the door shuddered under a powerful knock. I opened it to find Mac in the hallway, holding two bottles of Guinness, one of which he handed to me.

"Do you think she's coming back?" he asked, steamrolling into the room.

Mac didn't have to say her name. I knew he was talking about Jenny. Her absence from the set had been weighing heavily on all our minds. I had to wonder what she would have thought about seeing a mummified body tumble out of the wall today. No doubt, she would have taken it in stride.

"She didn't say she wasn't," I pointed out.

"That's something," Mac agreed, then took a swig of stout. "Why don't you call her, see how she's doing?"

"Damnit, Mac, I don't even have a cell phone number for her." Come to think of it, I wasn't even sure Jenny owned a cell phone. What kind of producer was I, anyway?

"You know that if she doesn't come back we're sunk, my friend," Mac said. He dropped into one of the chairs and shoved some papers aside so he could set his bottle on the motel work table. I snapped my computer shut in case his stout spilled and created yet another disaster for the show. I had been in the middle of updating our blog, describing the discovery of the body. It was the best I could do, since the police had confiscated Iggy's video. I was second-guessing myself about letting the deputy have that video—maybe I should have put up more of a fight—because that would have been something worth posting. Since Jenny's absence, there had been a slow but steady dip in the number of visitors to our site.

"She's coming back." I felt obligated to say it to Mac, the same way a general would reassure his troops that reinforcements were on the way, but deep down I wasn't so sure.

Jenny Cooper was the undisputed star of *Delmarva Renovators*. If it hadn't been for her, our little show would never have found its instant following on the Web. Much as I might like to think it was the camera work, the helpful home improvement hints, Mac's affable gruffness or even the interesting old foursquare I had chosen for our first project, I knew the driving force here was Jenny. She was not the typical middle-aged, flannel-shirt wearing, corny joke-cracking host you saw on some of the leading television home improvement shows. Jenny was worlds beyond that. She was sexy. Twenty-eight years old, raven-haired, blue-eyed, and with alabaster skin, her wardrobe tended toward skin-tight jeans and belly shirts. She made any red-blooded man take a second look. Put a cordless drill in her hand and a tool belt around her bare mid-riff, and Jenny Cooper became a home improvement goddess. Aphrodite with power tools.

Within a couple weeks, there was a buzz all across the world of renovators' blogs and chat rooms. Guys thought she was a babe. Girls saw her as cool, a hip chick who could wield power tools better than most men. It didn't hurt that Jenny came off tough as nails—which she was. Or so I'd thought until I'd gone and screwed things up. Screwed *Jenny*, that is, to put it in cruder terms.

Thanks to Jenny, *Delmarva Renovators* started to get more and more hits online. Tool companies called about sponsor-ships and advertising on the show. Several homeowners had e-mailed in hopes that *Delmarva Renovators* would tackle their old houses next, but we didn't have anything definite lined up after the

Cosden House. Even so, the show was really starting to build momentum. It was pretty exciting, considering that just one year ago, this whole enterprise had been nothing more than an idea Mac and I dreamt up over a few beers. Then Jenny had announced that she was taking some time off. I begged, I cajoled, stopping just short of threatening not to let her back on the show—that would have been the death of us, I was sure—but to no avail. Jenny walked off and disappeared with no way to get in touch with her and no word on how long she planned to be gone or where she was going. Tomorrow would be the fourth day.

To my surprise, I realized I had just sucked down the entire bottle of Guinness.

Mac was grinning. "Whoa, Hammer, you've still got the touch. Let me get you another one."

I noticed he was wearing a T-shirt that said: "Today's word is gigantic." Mac had a thing for T-shirts with sometimes outlandish sayings. At first, I'd thought they would be a bad idea on camera, but our viewers commented as much about the shirts as whatever project Mac was tackling on the video.

The room felt empty once Mac had gone. I don't suppose there's anything quite as lonely as a motel room. This one was standard issue—table, two chairs, TV bolted to the dresser and the bed where Jenny and I had our one-night stand. The pillows and bedspread seemed to glare at me, so I threw a pile of newspapers on the bed.

The clock radio sounded too tinny, so I switched on the TV hoping to get some music on VH1 or even MTV, but all they had were reality shows on losing weight and dating. One of these days I would have to download some songs onto my MacBook. If I ever found the time.

Chesapeake City itself had several comfortable B&Bs, but I had put up our crew in this motel off the interstate several miles away. The motel wasn't as posh, but it was far more economical. Every morning we got together in the parking lot and formed a mini-convoy for the twenty-minute ride to the jobsite. We headed back dog-tired at the end of a long day.

Briefly, I thought about calling my wife, Ellen. And just as quickly decided against it. I had already talked to her once today and that had been painful enough. She favored long, uncomfortable silences instead of arguing. It was a little like getting a letter that was nothing but a blank page. I think I would have preferred a bit more noise. The truth was, living away from home for several months was actually a trial separation, although neither Ellen nor I had opted to call it that. I never would have crossed the line with Jenny if my marriage hadn't been in a serious state of disrepair.

Talking to the kids had gone better. Josh was ten and still asked me when I was coming home. We went over his math homework on the phone. At twelve, Andrew had a better understanding of the chilly silence between mom and dad. We talked about his soccer team and the house project. Over spring break, he had spent a few days helping out at the house, mostly following Mac or Jenny around. He even had something of a crush on Jenny. I know his dad did. At his age it was harmless puppy love. Jenny pretended not to notice, but she treated him almost like a kid brother. She also taught him a lot about carpentry. By the time school started up again, Andrew could measure and cut, drill and hammer better than most grown men. I'd been proud of him, and I'd told him so. Just thinking about the boys made me feel better.

I took out the business card DFC Sullivan had given me. The number on the back was for a cell phone. I wasn't sure what to think about that. On the one hand, she'd said she was a renovator herself and wouldn't mind showing us her old house project. Then there were those playful blue eyes. Maybe she had noticed I wasn't wearing a wedding ring. I'd worn one up until we started the Cosden House, but I had taken it off, ostensibly telling myself it was for safety reasons. A lot of carpenters didn't wear rings because they tended to get hung up and could leave you with a mangled finger or hand. At the time, I hadn't given it much thought. Now I understood it was not only my way of launching our first big renovation project but also of starting to end thirteen years of marriage.

I slipped DFC Sullivan's card into my wallet, which was already bulging with half-forgotten business cards and scraps of paper.

The heavy stout had settled in my stomach like a load of liquid cement, mixing with all the plaster dust I had inhaled at the house earlier.

"You look worn out," Mac said, returning with the rest of the six-pack. "Try to remember to have some fun while we're at this. It's why you and I decided to give it a try in the first place."

I sighed and took a long drink. The Guinness reached out to give me a firm handshake. "Jenny or not, we've got a show to do," I said. "Looking at the glass half empty isn't going to help the situation."

Mac considered his empty bottle. "That's true, Hammer. But sometimes the beer runs out. Not much you can do about that."

There was a knock at the door. Mac got up to open it and Iggy came in carrying his laptop.

"I've got something I want to show you," Iggy said, setting the computer down on the work table. Without another word, he flipped open the laptop and played the video of the body tumbling out of the wall. He had edited out all the long pauses, so that we seemed to go right from the discovery to the police showing up in the space of a couple minutes. I saw Mac wince at the part where he broke off the corpse's finger. It was damn good stuff. Just the kind of thing that got you noticed on the Internet, a world that wasn't much different from a market square full of hucksters and street performers.

"But how—"

"I downloaded it to my laptop right away," he explained.

"That's why you weren't upset when the deputy confiscated your memory card."

He gave me a sly grin. "You can see that I already did an

edit. You want me to post it on our website?"

"You're going to piss off the police," Mac warned. "They might shut down the show."

"Without Jenny, the hits on our site have dropped way off," I said. "There isn't going to be any show if we don't land some major sponsors, and to do that we need people to watch. We need eyeballs."

"Just give me the word," Iggy said.

"Post it," I said, wondering if I had just put a nail in our show's coffin—or put us on the map.

In the morning, the crew of *Delmarva Renovators* made its usual convoy down to Chesapeake City. Iggy and Kat in the van, Mac driving the truck with me riding shotgun, and Marsha following in her Saab. There was plenty of room in one of the other vehicles, but Marsha drew the line at riding in pickup trucks or work vans. On more than one occasion, Marsha had made it clear that these vehicles ranked right up there with steel-toed boots—useful in their way but something to be avoided at all costs by the fashion-minded. Then, too, Marsha was forever running out somewhere to look at paint samples or swatches of fabric, so it made sense for her to keep her own vehicle handy.

Our first stop was for breakfast at the Bohemia Café. The small restaurant was at the corner of Second and George streets. Not as fancy as the other restaurants in town, it was more of a gathering spot for the locals. The $2.99 breakfast special featured two eggs, two slices of bacon, two slices of toast, and bottomless cups of coffee. Mac and I sat at the counter while the others squeezed into one of the booths along the wall. Like most of the locals, we all ordered the special.

Carl Batzer came over and poured coffee. "Did the police figure out yet who was in the wall of that house?" he asked.

"Not yet," I said, trying to be noncommittal. It was common knowledge that the Bohemia Café was the center of all gossip and actual news in Chesapeake City—although telling one from another was next to impossible. If you started a rumor over breakfast at the Bohemia Café it was all over town by lunchtime and sometimes made for an actual headline in the next day's county newspaper.

Pete Morrison was sitting at the counter, holding a cup of coffee in his paint-stained hands. He slid over to occupy the empty stool next to me and said *sotto voce*, "Some are saying it's Ezra Cosden himself. The ol' captain wanted to stay and watch over his family."

"Not unless he dyed his hair," I said. "That body had brown hair. Captain Cosden was ninety years old when he died. In the old pictures I've seen he had a full head of snowy hair."

Pretty much everything I knew about Captain Ezra Cosden had come from the tiny town museum operated by the Chesapeake City Historical Society. The exhibit on the captain consisted of a framed photograph with a paragraph of biographical information typed on a note card that was yellow with age and secured to the wall with a thumb tack.

Pete shrugged, then held out his coffee cup for a refill. "I also heard it might have been a business rival. They say ol' Captain Cosden didn't make his money playing fair and square."

"Careful what you go around saying," Carl said. "The Cosdens won't take kindly to hearing the captain run down."

"Maybe I heard that particular nugget from a Cosden," Pete said, raising his eyebrows in a knowing gesture.

"Who?"

"Let's just say it's someone from a side branch."

Carl shook his head. "Those Cosdens are like the royal family," he explained to me. "You've got your direct descendants of the captain and then you've got the descendants of his brothers and sisters. The direct ones like Edith Cosden think they're better than the others. Now, you know Rory Cosden? He's a side-brancher himself. But hell, he must have forty first cousins."

"They were all giving me some sour looks yesterday," I said.

"Blood runs thicker than water," Carl said, pronouncing the old saw with such gravity that it sounded like some distillation of real wisdom, kind of like the way he turned plain old hamburger into his famous Tuesday meatloaf special. Then he moved off to pour more coffee. At the sight of Carl's coffee pot, empty cups popped up like a nest of hungry baby birds.

Mac hadn't said anything because he was busy devouring the breakfast the waitress had put down in front of him. I had only picked at mine, and now the scrambled eggs were getting cold. I left them alone and made a sandwich out of the toast and bacon, washing it down with big gulps of coffee. I was anxious to get back on the job. All this talk about the body reminded me that we had a lot of work to do in the house itself. When we had left yesterday there was still plaster dust everywhere and rubble strewn across the floor—not to mention the pocket doors that still needed fixing.

"You going to eat those eggs?" Mac asked.

"Help yourself."

He slid the plate in front of him, dumped on what looked like half a bottle of Tabasco sauce, then shoveled them down.

On the other side of me, Pete stood up and left some bills on the counter. "Time for me to get back to work," he said. "The canvas calls."

"Much as you're in here, maybe you ought to set up a studio in the corner," I kidded him.

"Hey, I never said anything about being a *starving* artist," Pete said, grinning. "My muse gets cranky when she's hungry. Besides, what you told me about it not being Captain Cosden might just get me a free drink off somebody at Channel Cats tonight."

The others were finishing breakfast at the booth. We paid up and headed out to the street where we'd left our vehicles.

As we stood on the curb waiting to cross, I noticed the puzzled expression on Mac's face. Following his stare, I saw it too. The truck and van seemed to have melted into the pavement at a lopsided angle. It was soon clear why. We crossed the street to discover that someone had slashed the tires on the passenger side, where they would have been out of sight of the Bohemia Café's windows. Our vehicles sat hunched by the curb, the tires looking sad and deflated. At that moment, it was exactly how I felt.

Mac's face was turning red. He stood there clenching and unclenching his beefy fists. Iggy lit a cigarette and considered the vandalized vans the way he might have pondered a modernistic sculpture. Kat shivered and rubbed her arms. Marsha stalked over to her car, fuming. Her tires had been left alone—maybe whoever it was had run out of time—but a deep scratch cut through the silver paint from the front fender to the back bumper. On her shiny Saab, the ugly mark stood out like a wound.

"If I didn't know better, I'd say someone was trying to send us a message," I said.

CHAPTER 4

I wasn't about to let some flat tires put us any further behind schedule. The Cosden House was only two blocks away, so we took what we needed out of the van and lugged it to the jobsite. Most of our tools were already there, waiting for us. Marsha drove Kat over in her car—the kid was a little more shaken up than the rest of us. Iggy stayed with the truck and van.

I called over to the local garage but was told they were too busy to send anyone over. After I got off the phone, I remembered that the garage was owned by a Cosden. If the slashed tires and vandalism to Marsha's car hadn't been enough, it began to occur to me that we had somehow succeeded in ticking off the extended Cosden clan. I also noticed that nobody came out of the café across the street to help—or to offer advice and opinions, which I had learned was a popular pastime in Chesapeake City. Normally, if you so much as raked leaves you'd have five or six people stop by to instruct you on the finer points of leaf raking. No, the locals wanted to keep out of this one because they would still be living here long after our amusing little show had packed up and moved on. They were staying on the townie side of the fence.

Gritting my teeth, I practically stabbed at the buttons on my cell phone. After a few more calls, I finally found a tow truck all the way up in the county seat, so that was going to take a while.

Mac and I trundled more tools over to the Cosden House.

"If I catch the smart ass who did this—"

"Don't even tell me," I said. "I don't want to be an accessory to murder."

Try as I might, I couldn't really summon a healthy dose of rage over the slashed tires. And Mac looked angry enough for both of us. Mostly, I felt sad. Up until yesterday—even until we walked out of the Bohemia Café—Chesapeake City had seemed like one of those fortunate places where bad things never happened. This was a town where most people still didn't bother to lock their doors. The town's tourist appeal made it feel like an enclave insulated from crime. I could see now that I had suffered from wishful thinking wrapped up in naiveté, not unlike one of those party appetizers where a toothpick pins a strip of bacon around a scallop. Tasty, irresistible and ultimately not all that healthy. It didn't take a genius to figure out that our discovery of the body had changed everything.

"I wonder about you sometimes, Hammer. You ought to be good and pissed off right about now. You're acting way too calm."

"We're here to get a job done and produce our show, which is exactly what we're going to do."

"Who the hell would slash our tires?" Mac demanded. "It's not like we killed anybody."

"Mac, did you ever consider that whoever knew about the body in the wall is letting us know they aren't happy that we found it?" *They're probably even less thrilled that we posted it on the Internet,* I silently added.

"Then let's hope there aren't any more bodies," he said. "Because I'd hate to see what they slash next. These are some ugly people we're dealing with."

As we walked, the town around us seemed to have changed. There were still the same old houses, the same people on the streets, but I didn't think I could ever look at any of them in quite the same way.

Even to call Chesapeake City a town was something of a stretch. Its nickname, Canal Town, seemed a better fit. The town fathers had come up with the outsized name Chesapeake City in a fit of early nineteenth century ambition. Before that, it had been known as Bohemia Village—and in truth, it was still a village today of about three hundred houses around a grid of streets and the waterfront. The majority of houses dated to the 1840s and 1850s, when the town had undergone boom times with the growing importance of the Chesapeake and Delaware Canal. The fourteen-mile canal through the heart of the Delmarva Peninsula connected the Chesapeake and Delaware bays, creating a shorter shipping route between Baltimore and Philadelphia. Because the two bays were actually at different elevations, when the canal opened in 1829 a series of locks, like water-filled stair steps, were needed to carry vessels up and down between the two bodies of water.

One of the locks was in Chesapeake City at the midpoint of the canal. Farmers brought their grain, tomatoes, watermelons and corn to Chesapeake City, where it was loaded onto barges or sailing ships for transport to the big cities. The town was also a stopping point for the Ericsson steamers that carried passengers between Philadelphia and Baltimore. You could catch the steamer for the big city here, or else stop for a meal or a drink if you were just passing through.

The town grew. Substantial homes owned by ship captains and lumber barons went up within sight of the canal, some of them with three floors, second-story porches and widow's walks. Captain Ezra Cosden had been one of the last such men to build along the canal after the turn of the previous century.

Along with these big houses, homes for canal workers and their families began to go up along the narrow streets. Most of these houses were nothing fancy, just cottages really, with no more for a foundation than some local stone stacked dry or just four stout logs directly on the ground. They followed a similar pattern of two rooms downstairs, a side hall with staircase, and a lean-to kitchen at the back. Two or three bedrooms upstairs. The wood came from scraps left by the lumbermen or barges dismantled in town. It was a tradition to paint many of these old barges in bright colors—purple, robin's egg blue, even pink—and when the barge boards were used as siding the frugal homeowners didn't bother to re-paint the wood. As a result, Chesapeake City had a legacy of cottages painted all the colors of the rainbow. The tradition had returned with the town's renaissance and the tourists loved it.

Over time, the town's fortunes had ebbed and flowed like the tides on the canal. The middle years of the twentieth century would prove especially hard on Chesapeake City. In 1919, the United States government purchased the canal from its private owners and began deepening and widening the waterway. The locks were removed to make it a sea-level canal. There was a strategic purpose behind the government project. During World War I, a new weapon—the German U-boat— had wreaked havoc on the U.S. merchant fleet in coastal waters. In response, the government created an intracoastal waterway that would protect merchant ships by keeping them out of the open sea where the U-boats prowled.

With the lock gone, the town lost its importance as a port. Large sea-going ships now passed on the new intracoastal waterway but they did not stop, though the town was still a center for shipping local produce. Also, the state highway passed right through town as it crossed the new lift bridge. The town had gas stations, a movie theater, a soda-bottling plant, general stores and a butcher shop. The canal had changed, but no one seemed too worried about the town's future.

Then came the shipwreck that would doom the town, though nobody knew it at the time. On a fall day in 1942, a merchant ship called the *SS Franz Klassen* went off course and struck the lift bridge across the canal, reducing it to twisted wreckage. Considering that the ship was a captured German vessel converted to U.S. service, the rumors flew that it was a case of Nazi espionage—though many pointed out that German secret agents most likely would have found a better target than the Chesapeake City lift bridge. The bridge was not immediately replaced because resources were needed elsewhere during wartime. For the next seven years, crossing the canal required climbing aboard the *Gotham*, a double-deck ferry boat that had once been used in New York's harbor. A smaller ferry boat carried passengers only—including children to school. Old-timers still recalled those days of riding the ferry with a twinkle of nostalgia in their eye.

The new state highway bridge was completed in 1949. It was a gleaming, mile-long marvel with an arch that soared more than two hundred fifty feet above the surface of the canal. The day that bridge opened and cars no longer came through town was the day that Chesapeake City began to die. The town that had once been a hub for commerce on the canal and then on the state highway now found that it had been bypassed.

It was a slow death. The colorful paint on the cottages peeled. Shutters fell off the big houses. Nor'easters roared down the canal to strip off shingles that were not replaced. Shops and small businesses closed. Houses fell into disrepair as families moved on to towns with more opportunity. By the mid-1970s Chesapeake City could have been a stand-in for an Old West ghost town. The only place that seemed to flourish was a biker bar known as The Hole in the Wall, in an old house by the canal. It was so tough that one time when a deputy went in to break up a fight, the patrons stole his patrol car.

And then came a flood tide of change. A group of history-minded renovators formed a partnership and started buying up the old houses and restoring them. A wealthy heiress lent her endless money and enthusiasm to the cause. The sight of a single renewed cottage on a street had a domino effect. Renovators bought up the next one and the next one. The town established an historic district and several homes were listed with the Maryland Historical Trust. Now, nearly thirty years after the first fresh paint had appeared, there were just three houses in town that had not undergone fairly substantial restoration and renewal. The Cosden House was one of the holdouts.

Nowadays, Chesapeake City's real estate market remained steady, even after the housing bubble had burst everywhere else. Most houses had at least some water view, and there were shops and great restaurants all within walking distance. Baby boomers with deep pockets fell in love with the place and moved mountains to live there. The down side was that town natives found themselves priced out even as they were glad to see the town they loved restored. And yet, the town was still relatively undiscovered, just far enough from the big cities to be beyond easy commuting distance. It all seemed like a perfect location for *Delmarva Renovators*.

That is, it had up until twenty-four hours ago.

"Uh oh," said Mac as we came in sight of our project house. For once, Mac was wearing his glasses. He was peering at the front porch, where a couple stood waiting. "The homeowners are here."

CHAPTER 5

Considering that this day was already going downhill, the arrival of the homeowners meant that the incline had just gotten steeper. Chip and Cindy Pritchard stood on the front porch staring at the yellow crime scene tape tacked across the front door. "I didn't expect to see you two here," I said, trying to keep my tone light, even though, in my head, I was hearing something like that piercing warning beep just before the burglar alarm goes off.

"We got up this morning and decided to take a drive out to see what's going on with the house. We just sent out a bunch of invitations to Canal Day so we're really hoping the house is done by then." Chip paused. "What's up with the tape? Did you just stain the floors or something? That ought to keep people from walking on them. Crime scene, huh? That's a good one. Pretty effective."

"Actually, the police put that up," I said.

"On account of the body," Mac added helpfully. When I tried to glare at him out of the corner of my eye, I noticed his T-shirt said "I'M BIG IN EUROPE."

Cindy clutched her chest. "My God, was there a murder?"

"Not a murder exactly," I said in my calmest voice, hoping to keep things on an even keel. "At least, not a murder that took place in this century."

Chip stared at me as if he wasn't quite sure what to think.

He had a long, lean face that reminded me of a hunting dog; in fact, he was now quivering like a springer spaniel that had spotted its prey. That description didn't quite do him justice, however. He was a handsome guy who looked as if he had just stepped out of a J. Crew catalog with his equally attractive wife on his arm. You know the type—used to getting his way because he was better looking and a whole lot richer than you.

Chip had all the traits of a banker or a lawyer—which, in fact, he used to be. But Chip had given up his law practice to make what he called "real money." Not that he'd been having trouble making ends meet as a junior partner at a D.C. law firm. When we first met, I'd heard the story of how, on evenings and weekends, he had done a lot of research into service franchises. He had then taken a big chunk out of his 401(k) and bought a franchise called "Doody Calls." As in dog doody. It was not, at first glance, anything that seemed all that promising or glamorous. But the Pritchards now had a fleet of vehicles that visited yards in the greater Washington metropolitan area to clean up after Fido and Fifi on behalf of other professionals who were just too busy or who deemed doody detail to be beneath them. The Pritchards' franchise received a monthly fee from all those customers, which enabled them to afford a high-end BMW and to bankroll the renovation of the Cosden House. As Chip liked to point out, "We're not picking up dog poop. We're picking up *money*."

The thought made me smile. Oops. Chip was glaring at me. *Big* Oops.

"Someone was murdered in our house," he said. "Is that supposed to be *funny?*"

"No, it's not funny at all," I said. "It's just that what I'm trying to tell you is that this isn't a real crime scene. This isn't going to slow us down at all."

I glanced at Mac, who rolled his eyes. Mac was always accusing me of being a hopeless optimist, and maybe in this case he was right.

"Will somebody please explain what the hell is going on,"

Chip demanded.

Quickly, I gave the Pritchards a rundown of what we knew. They took it better than I thought they might. I was pleasantly surprised to see that the Pritchards were warming to the idea that there was something mysterious about their house.

"You could have called us," Chip reprimanded me, his voice still taut. "It was a very unpleasant surprise to drive all the way out here this morning only to discover that our house is a crime scene."

"I can imagine," I said, working hard to hit the proper tone of contrition. "I have to apologize. I really did plan to call you this morning, just as soon as we knew what was going on with the police."

"It's been crazy around here," Mac added.

It was about to get crazier. As we stood there talking, an un-marked police car pulled up to the curb. I felt a nervous stirring in my stomach when I saw DFC Maureen Sullivan at the wheel. She was long-limbed and graceful as she climbed out of her Crown Victoria. I also couldn't help but notice the sharp creases of her uniform and the gleaming gun belt around her waist. She set a broad-brimmed hat on her head and was utterly transformed into a figure of authority.

We all stood on the porch watching her approach. "You didn't wear your painting clothes," I said.

DFC Sullivan favored me with a smile. On second thought, that uniform made her kind of sexy. My stomach did another little flip. What was I, sixteen years old? "I'll help you paint if you bring your crew over to my place for a day. How 'bout that?"

"Sounds like a deal to me."

Chip Pritchard stepped forward. "You must be here to take down the crime scene tape."

"And who might you be?" DFC Sullivan asked, all business again.

He introduced himself and Cindy as the property owners. "We really need you to let them get back to work," he said.

"I'm not sure I can do that," the deputy said.

"Why not?" Chip's voice rose an octave.

"At this point, the state police are handling the investigation," DFC Sullivan said. "It's their call, Mr. Pritchard, not mine."

"This is ridiculous," Chip said. "How long do we have to wait to go back in our house?"

DFC Sullivan didn't answer but excused herself and walked back to her patrol car while we stood on the front porch, wondering what was next.

"Maybe she's calling the paddy wagon," Mac said.

The Pritchards glared at him. Mac just shrugged.

The deputy was back in a few minutes. "I made some calls," she said. "The state police said it's okay to go back in as long as you don't work in the room where the body was found."

"Oh God," Cindy groaned. "I just thought of something. Now we'll probably have a ghost. We'll have to hire an exorcist or whatever they're called. You know, to get rid of unquiet spirits."

"If we do anything, honey, we're going to sue the real estate agent," Chip said.

The deputy shook her head. "That body has been in the wall for decades," she said. "I doubt very much that your real estate agent knew anything about it. I'd say hardly anyone knew. Generally, when you hide a body in a wall, you want to keep quiet about it."

"What about the Cosdens?" I asked.

"That might be another story," she said. "Now step aside, people, and let me take down this tape."

She quickly pulled off the tape as we stood by like we were watching someone unwrap a birthday present. I unlocked the front door and in we went. The house felt cold and the air tasted of dust. Our footsteps rang on the bare wood floors, echoing under the tall ceilings. The Pritchards shook their heads as Mac pointed through the dining room doorway to where the body had tumbled out yesterday. The state police had taken away the bundle of old clothes and limp hair, but in my mind's eye I could still see the lips curled back in a grin.

"Home sweet home," Mac concluded. "Let's get to work."

"We can't do anything in the dining room," I reminded him.

"There's plenty of work in the kitchen. For starters, we can finish putting down the subfloor." Mac went off into the kitchen.

DFC Sullivan looked around from face to face. "Aren't you missing somebody?" she asked.

"Our cameraman is waiting for a tow truck," I said. "We had a problem this morning."

"Someone vandalized our vehicles," Marsha said.

The deputy's eyebrows went up. "Oh? And when were you going to tell me this?"

I wished Marsha hadn't said anything, but it was too late now. The last thing I wanted to do was involve us any deeper with the police than we already were. In fact, I was doing my best to forget all about the slashed tires, hoping that was the end of it. But now I was on the spot, considering that the Pritchards had overheard and stood nearby, listening to my explanation.

"Someone slashed the tires on Mac's pickup truck and our work van this morning while they were parked across from the Bohemia Café," I said. "This same someone also took a knife to the paint job on Marsha's car."

"Oh great," Chip put in. "Have you got into some kind of small-town feud? Things like that don't happen in a place like this."

DFC Sullivan held up a hand to quiet him, which made the Doggy Doo King look annoyed. "Slashed how many tires?" she asked.

"Two on each side. That makes four altogether. We were inside having breakfast and didn't see a thing."

"Were you going to report this?"

"What would be the point?"

"You've been working here for months without any trouble," she answered. "Then yesterday you find a body in the house and this morning your tires get slashed. You think maybe the two events are connected?"

"Why am I getting the impression that this is a rhetorical question?"

Mac had reappeared in the doorway. "First rule of police work is that there's no such thing as coincidence."

DFC Sullivan nodded. "Consider this reported," she said.

I stood there exchanging a long gaze with the deputy. It was what you might call an awkward silence.

"Come on, Hammer," Mac said in a stage whisper. "We've got to look busy for the homeowners."

DFC Sullivan smiled. The Pritchards did not look amused, but they clumped off to inspect the work that had been done over the last few days. Truth was, there hadn't been a whole lot of progress since their last visit. The dining room was a wreck, although we had fished more electrical wires through the walls and patched some of the cracked plaster. Progress was slow since we'd been missing our star carpenter. If the pace didn't pick up soon we were going to need additional help.

"You ever do any carpentry work when you aren't keeping law and order?" I asked DFC Sullivan.

To my surprise, she actually seemed to consider it, cocking her head to one side. Then she shook her head. "I'm strictly a do-it-yourselfer in that department, Mr. Martell," she said. "I've learned a lot about working on houses, but what you need around here is a pro."

"Tell me about it." Not for the first time, it occurred to me that *Delmarva Renovators* was in trouble if we couldn't come up with a good carpenter. Jenny had really left us in the lurch. If she didn't return in a day or two, I was seriously going to have to consider finding some new on-air talent. "And by the way, you can just call me Tom."

"Hey, Tommy, could I get some help in here?" Mac called from the kitchen.

"I'd better let you get to work," DFC Sullivan said.

"Thanks for letting us in."

She hooked her thumbs in her gun belt. "Well, you know where to find me if you need me."

I couldn't help watching her fine figure as she walked out. I reminded myself that I still had DFC Sullivan's number in my wallet. But I was still a married man. Sort of. And then there was Jenny—

"Hammer!" Mac called from the kitchen.

I grabbed my tool belt and went to help.

The kitchen at the Cosden House was now a bare room stripped to the studs. It used to have multiple layers of wall-paper and paint on the walls, which we might have saved if the kitchen hadn't needed new wiring and plumbing to replace that scary knob-and-tube electrical system and the leaky copper pipes. We had wanted to preserve the original plaster hidden under the ceiling tiles, but that was gone now too for the same reasons. Sometimes it was easier just to start over. The fifteen by seventeen room was now a blank slate.

Getting it to that point wasn't easy. The demolition of the walls and ceiling was dusty, messy work. We ripped out the old white enamel sink, the cast iron radiator, and the cheap Formica counter tops someone had installed thirty or forty years ago. The kitchen cabinets went too. They were a hodge-podge of plastic-coated particle board and cheap metal cabinets gone rusty. Nothing at all worth saving. Whenever I worked on an old house, I tried not to be too critical of the work that had come before. I'm sure the Cosdens had done the best they could with their old kitchen on a limited budget and before the advent of the Big Box home improvement stores made plentiful and affordable options available. The junk we had ripped out was probably the only stuff for sale at the hardware store in the county seat three decades ago.

The floor was our biggest challenge. There was original wood beneath, but it was buried under a layer of industrial-strength asbestos tiles that would have been more at home in a school cafeteria. Beneath the tiles was an original linoleum floor in a red-and-black checkerboard pattern.

Asbestos was a problem. If I'd been doing the work on my own home, I would have closed off the kitchen doorways with plastic sheets, donned a respirator, kept the tiles wet and gone to work with a long-handled scraper. In other words, I would have been as safe as possible without going overboard. But on a project like this that was very much in the public eye, we had decided to call in a licensed asbestos removal contractor. That job alone, which two suited-up guys did in one day, took a two-thousand dollar chunk out of our budget. However, it did make for what I thought was an interesting episode that highlighted the expensive problem of asbestos in old homes.

Now we were finally down to bare wood.

"You measure, I'll cut," said Mac.

"What's our motto?"

"Measure twice, cut once, hope for the best."

"I wish we could have done something with this old flooring." When we had finally uncovered the pine floorboards, I had tried without success to talk the Pritchards into refinishing the original wood.

"The homeowners want tile, they get tile," Mac said with a shrug.

The trick now was to get the floor nice and solid so that over time the vibrations wouldn't crack the grout or the tiles themselves. That was a challenge in an old house like this. Down in the basement we had tightened up the floor joists as much as possible. The original wood floor made a good foundation, but we added a quarter-inch cement board underlayment. That and the tile would put the kitchen floor higher than in the rest of the house, but that was something a threshold could fix.

One drawback of tile floors was that they were cold. We had already taken care of that problem by installing radiant heating. Tubing stapled up between the floor joists was filled with hot water from an auxiliary heating system. It would be pretty sweet to have warm tiles under your toes when you came downstairs to make your coffee on a winter's morning. It was also expensive to set up the system, but that was what the homeowners wanted.

Mac and I worked until lunchtime cutting plywood for the subfloor, then gluing and nailing it down. By the time we got done, Mac could jump up and down without the wood so much as making a creak or groan. That floor was solid.

Iggy showed up to film us putting in the last piece of plywood. He told us that a tow truck had finally arrived. The driver was able to fix Mac's pickup on the spot with some plugs for the tires, but the van's tires were more seriously damaged and would have to be replaced. It was now on the back of a Jerdan truck, being taken to the garage.

Kat arrived with our lunch order from The Hole in the Wall, our second eatery of choice. It was the tavern downstairs from the more upscale Bayard House Restaurant. By now, she knew what everyone wanted, from Mac's roast beef on rye to Marsha's salad. She put the box with the sandwiches in the middle of our pristine new subfloor and we all had a kind of picnic, using milk crates and five-gallon buckets of joint compound for seating. Even the Pritchards joined in. They seemed jazzed by the progress in the kitchen taking place right before their very eyes. How could they realize we were falling further and further behind schedule? I wasn't about to ruin their good spirits by filling them in. All through lunch Cindy and Marsha chatted about room colors and what sort of tile to use in the bathroom.

"You going to eat that pickle?" Chip asked Mac, pointing at the slice of dill on his sandwich wrapping.

"You want to arm wrestle me for it?"

Chip blinked a couple of times like he was trying to decide if Mac was serious. "Never mind," he finally said. He looked around the room as if taking inventory, then asked, "Where's Jenny, by the way?"

"She had some personal business to take care of," I said. "She'll be back in a day or two."

"That's good. You'd really be up a creek without Jenny." Chip laughed. "You'd never get this house done on time!"

"Yup," I said.

Mac bit down so hard on his pickle we could all hear it crunch. The next sound we heard was the front window shattering.

CHAPTER 6

The brick lay in a puddle of broken glass on the living room floor. Mac charged out the front door while the rest of us just gawked at the jagged hole in the window like bystanders at a train wreck. I think we had all worked so long and so hard on the Cosden House that the place felt like an old friend. To see the house willfully damaged was painful—like we had been the ones hit with a brick. I toed at the broken glass, feeling at a loss.

There were actually three windows facing the street, a huge double-hung flanked by narrower lights on either side. Like all the other windows in the house, the top part of the double-hungs had craftsman-style grids with sixteen individual "lights" or panes made of wavy antique glass. The brick had come right through the bottom half of the center window. I said a silent prayer of relief that the brick hadn't damaged any of the delicate and irreplaceable craftsman-era muntins. Even so, it would take a great deal of painstaking work with linseed oil, glazing compound and a putty knife to replace the glass.

Mac came back in, red-faced with anger. "Not a soul in sight," he growled. "I wish whoever is doing this would show himself. I'm getting pretty damn sick of it."

"This is getting out of hand," Marsha agreed.

By itself, I could have dismissed the tire-slashing incident as an expensive prank, maybe even the handiwork of the bored teenagers who sometimes hung out on the granite steps of the old bank building on the corner. Of course, those teens would have been in school this morning. But sending a brick through the window made it clear that these were acts of malice. It made me uneasy to think that there was an adult or adults in this village capable of acting that way.

"First the tires, now the house," Mac said. "What next?"

The Pritchards looked at each other, then at me. Chip said, "This is about the body you found in the wall, isn't it?"

"We don't know that."

"Sure it is," Chip said, his eyes narrowing. They were tawny-colored, like a cat's. "You work here for months without any trouble and then in one day someone vandalizes your vehicles *and* throws a brick through the window. *My* window. You're seriously telling me that you don't think there's a connection with the body?"

Deep down, I knew he was right. Chip hadn't made a fortune in the dog waste removal industry by being dense. The problem was that I didn't know what to do about the situation. As the show's producer and de facto head honcho on this old house project, I was supposed to be the one with all the answers. Need a permit? Tom will get one. Camera on the fritz? Ask Tom about it. Town manager on the phone? Somebody get Tom. I could deal with all those daily crises with one hand tied behind my back. But at the moment, I didn't have any good answers as to what we had done to make someone in town angry to the point that they would destroy property.

"You need to call the police," Chip insisted. "You need to get to the bottom of this right away, before something worse happens."

Marsha approached the brick, glass crunching underfoot. She poked at it with the toe of her stylish boot and rolled it over. "Take a look at this," she said.

Scratched into the brick was a name. The letters were shaky and not very deep, as if they had been done in a hurry.

"Who in the world," Marsha said, "is Leo Cosden?"

I didn't know either, but I could make a pretty good guess. And I knew just where I could find the answer.

The Chesapeake City Historical Society and Museum was located in Franklin Hall, a three-story brick structure in the heart of the town's historic district. Built in 1878, the building had been home to many uses and causes over the years: Masonic hall, arts council, town library, various shops and businesses, even a butcher's shop in the cellar at the turn of the previous century. (It was the Mason's who had named it after one of their own, Benjamin Franklin.) The building was owned by the town's historical society, which, I had learned, was constantly struggling to pay for the upkeep of Franklin Hall. Even in the short time that *Delmarva Renovators* had been in town, the historical society had spent more than one hundred thousand dollars to have the building's foundation overhauled. Our show had taken time to film the masons as they worked to remove the old mortar between the foundation stones and then painstakingly repoint the cellar walls with an historically correct mortar mixture. To use modern Portland cement would not only have been a travesty, but it might have cracked the original field stone.

Iver Jones was president of the historical society and self-appointed museum curator. As museums went, the Smithsonian it was not. Worn blue carpeting covered the floor and the walls held a collage of black-and-white photographs, old maps, yellowed newspaper clippings and the occasional "artifact"—such as the Civil War sword carried by Captain Ezra Cosden's father. The leap in time and events from one square foot of wall to another had an effect that was a little like being trapped in an elevator that stopped at random floors. However, the quirky nature of the museum was part of its charm, and on first coming to town I had spent hours reading everything on the walls and poring over the local history books.

In theory, the museum was self-guided, but nine times out of ten visitors received a personal tour from Iver. His antiques shop was located just across the street in one of Chesapeake City's oldest houses. No sooner would someone walk into the museum than Iver would pop in after them. Those who knew Iver said these personal tours weren't motivated as much by his love of history as they were by the fear that a tourist would walk off with something valuable, such as the program from the fire company's seventieth anniversary banquet back in 1981.

I didn't have to wait long for Iver to appear. He must have been keeping watch from behind the lacy curtains of his antiques shop. Even though I'd been in town now for several months, he still didn't trust me alone in "his" museum.

"What can I help you with today, Tom?" he asked, drifting through the museum door with all the grace of a dancer. Iver was on the short side and lean, quite the opposite of what his robust Nordic name might suggest. "Iver" was the sort of moniker that seemed to suit a Viking better than the effete owner of an antiques shop. Other than a few strands of blond still evident in his white hair, Iver bore little resemblance to a Viking. It was hard to know Iver's exact age, but I was pretty sure he could see seventy-five in his rearview mirror. Iver was a direct descendant of the Swedish settlers who had arrived on what was now the Delaware coast in 1638, and he never failed to let that fact slip in the first five minutes of any conversation with a newcomer.

He did not put on airs when it came to his appearance. Iver wore jeans, off-brand sneakers, and a green hoodie that featured a leaping rockfish and the slogan: "Hooked on Chesapeake City!" Iver's wardrobe usually consisted of whatever sweatshirts and T-shirts he picked up at the end-of-season sales in the gift shops in town. There were several such shops that catered to the tourists, selling everything from those T-shirts to tchotchkes like ceramic frogs with the slogan "Hop on over to Canal Town" and coffee mugs with pictures of the soaring

Chesapeake City bridge on them. Iver would sniff in a superior way at Merchant Association meetings as he pointed out that he sold *antiques*. And it was true that he had a high-end shop that drew buyers from a wide area, though lately the Internet had been taking its toll on his in-store sales. He was very interested in our renovation project, because the Pritchards had been good customers, buying up several local pieces for the house—if and when it was ever finished.

"Just the person I was looking for," I said. It paid to butter up Iver like an ear of corn, since he held the keys to all those locked filing cabinets filled with town records. "I could use your expert help."

He shot me a look and set one hand on his out-thrust hip, a move that would have suited an actress in an old black-and-white movie. The butter must have been a little thick, even for Iver. "This must be a good one."

"Oh, it is," I said. "What can you tell me about Leo Cosden?"

"Brother to Captain Ezra Cosden," Iver said right off the bat. He really was like a walking encyclopedia of town history. "He was a captain himself. Drowned in Chesapeake Bay when his ship went down during a storm. I thought you would have known about him."

Iver somehow managed to make one's lack of historical knowledge seem to be a serious personal shortcoming, like leaving home without your pants. "Do you have any other information about him?" I asked. "Were there any newspaper accounts of what happened?"

"Well, we may be able to find something. But I *am* supposed to be running my shop. I guess I could spare a few minutes. What's so important about Leo Cosden all of a sudden?"

"About twenty minutes ago someone threw a brick through our front window," I explained. "Leo's name was scratched on it."

Iver didn't so much as blink. "In that case, I can see where it's possibly worth looking him up."

I followed him deeper into the museum. The front half of Franklin Hall was rented for shops—selling jewelry and more tchotchkes—but the back half that held the museum had a mysterious air, with tiny rooms hiding off hallways and steps leading down to a cellar that seemed to go on and on. Depending on your point of view, the cellar held either priceless antiques and town mementos, or else piles of rusting and mildewed junk. It really depended on how one viewed the intrinsic value of everything from ferry landing signs to milk bottles from the long-gone Losten's Dairy just outside town.

"How much do you know about Leo Cosden?" I asked.

"Not much," Iver said. "He died around a hundred years ago. It's his brother, Ezra, who's the famous one. You do know about *him*, don't you? You *are* working on his house, although I understand not everyone is happy about it."

Iver must have heard about the slashed tires. News got around this town faster than a stray cat finds a fish bone. I glanced at my tour guide and wondered how long it would be before everyone knew I'd been asking about Leo, the other Cosden. Iver was a notorious gossip.

We climbed a set of creaky stairs. From my previous visits, I knew that the second floor of the museum was off limits to the public. Not that anyone could have gotten far anyway. It was crammed so full of boxes and filing cabinets that I stepped gingerly onto the floor, half afraid that my weight would be all it took to finally collapse the building.

Every time an old person died in Chesapeake City and the relatives cleaned out the attic, Iver was famous for interceding as the boxes headed for the local landfill. They wound up jammed into the second floor instead. These boxes held photographs of long-dead relatives, outdated legal papers, old newspapers. Anything that seemed especially important ended up stuffed for safekeeping into one of the cubbyholes under the eaves.

Iver led the way, switching on low-wattage bulbs that barely cut through the gloom. Blinds covered the dormer windows to

keep out the deteriorating effects of sunlight. He was sur-
prisingly agile as he slipped down the narrow walkways
between the stacks, almost like a spider dancing down a web.
Dust swirled up and made my nostrils twitch. The second floor
smelled of old paper, mildew and mice. Something touched my
face and I recoiled, then realized it was only a cobweb.

"That's the late eighteen hundreds over there," Iver said,
gesturing toward a corner. "The early nineteen hundreds are
right here. Great Depression in that pile by the back corner."

"Where do you keep the Ark of the Covenant?" I wondered. "Right behind the Holy Grail?"

Iver didn't dignify that with an answer. His organizational
system might have worked for him, but to me it was all just a
jumble of boxes and filing cabinets. We stopped in front of a
pint-sized doorway into a cubbyhole. A brass padlock secured
the door. A heavy key ring appeared from a deep pocket in the
rockfish sweatshirt. Iver was full of surprises. He began flipping through the keys and muttering in a way that reminded
me of the old nuns fingering their rosary beads back when I
was an altar boy.

"Let's try this one," he said, fitting a key to the padlock. He
grunted with the effort of trying to turn it. When the lock
didn't open, he went back to the key ring until he found
another likely suspect. This time, the lock popped free. He
opened the door to reveal the dark depths of a cubbyhole.
"This is where I keep the Cosdens," Iver said. He cleared her
throat. "The Cosden family papers, I mean."

"Okay," I said. "That's a start."

"Go on in and bring out a couple of boxes," he said. "Let's
see what we can find."

I had to stoop down to get inside the cubbyhole. I felt
around for a light switch. Nothing. Not even a pull cord for an
overhead bulb. It was good and dark in there.

"Iver, have you got a flashlight or something? I can't see a
thing."

"Go on, you're a big boy. You're not afraid of a few spiders, are you?"

Well, yeah, as a matter of fact. But it wasn't like I could expect Iver to haul the boxes out. He was spry enough, but he was an old man. And he took pleasure in ordering people around. I ducked lower and felt my way into the darkness. Just enough light spilled in that I could make out the edges of the boxes stacked inside. And there were enough spider webs in there to weave a parachute out of the silk.

"What am I looking for?"

"Don't worry, you're not even close."

I inched forward. This must be how cave explorers felt. My knees kept running into my elbows as I shuffled inside. I blinked, trying to get used to the darkness. The tiny room felt like it was holding its breath. Something way back in the corner rustled. Crickets, I told myself. Mice.

Let's get something straight here, okay? I'm not a total wimp. Mice, bugs, bats and snakes don't bother me much. Spiders, on the other hand, are a different story. I loathe anything with eight legs. Hey, I know arachnids do a lot of good, catching insects and all that, but there's nothing lovable about them. Glancing once more at the veil of webs, I had a reassuring thought that black widows preferred lairs with more air and sunlight. On the other hand, the place was just right for a brown recluse.

"You have to go farther," Iver said. "The box I want is toward the back."

Then maybe you ought to crawl in here and get it. But I kept my thoughts to myself and crept deeper into the cubbyhole. Looking over my shoulder, I could just see Iver's silhouette in the open doorway. In my mind's eye I could imagine him shutting the door and snapping that big lock shut. I had another crazy notion, which was that I really didn't know much about Iver. He might even be a Cosden himself, way back somewhere in his family tree. This town seemed to be full of twisted family roots.

I regretted not telling anyone I was coming here. Nobody

would come looking for me anytime soon in a forgotten cubbyhole on the second floor of the Chesapeake City Historical
Society. When they finally got around to unlocking the door I
would be a twin to the mummy that tumbled out of the wall at
the Cosden House. Maybe they could put me in one of the
glass display cases downstairs like a relic from a circus side-
show, or maybe a warning to other meddlesome outsiders.

Pushing that thought from my mind, I grabbed a box and
started toward the doorway. I tossed it out and started back for
another. My head got a good whack against the low ceiling
when I forgot to duck. The impact brought down a nest of
cobwebs that stuck to my face like shrink wrap. Something
lively scurried across my shoulder. It took a real effort not to
go running out right then and there—OK, I'll admit it, *running
like a little girl*—but Iver would have gleefully spread that story
around town by suppertime. Even an arachnophobe has his
pride. *Leo Cosden, you'd better be worth it.* I took a deep breath
and tried to forget about the spiders as I dragged out another
box.

Iver had started rummaging through the boxes. By the time
I carried out a fifth box, he was waving a piece of paper at me.

"This is it," he announced, unfolding an old newspaper
clipping. Someone had penciled a date at the top. October 20,
1913. Oddly enough, the newsprint wasn't nearly as brown and
brittle as might be expected. In fact, it was in pretty good
shape. I knew that was because old newsprint contained a higher percentage of "rag content"—actual cotton fibers. Books
and newspapers today were all wood pulp and chemicals,
which was why they turned brown so quickly. However, it
wasn't the quality of the paper I was interested in so much as
the events of ninety-plus years ago.

"What does it say?"

"Do you expect me to do everything!" Iver snapped. I
didn't let it bother me—Iver was famously cranky and overly
dramatic, but his bark was worse than his bite. He sighed. "The
fact is that I left my cheaters in the shop. My eyes are getting

old, Tom. You can read it for yourself."

With Iver looking over my shoulder, that's just what I did.

CHAPTER 7

When I got back to the Cosden House, someone had swept up the glass and patched the broken window with cardboard and duct tape. Not fancy, but effective. From the street, the missing pane gave the house an appearance of having a gap-toothed smile.

Mac was finishing up the subfloor in the kitchen with some help from Chip Pritchard. I was more than a little amazed to see our homeowner down on his hands and knees with a cordless drill, securing the cement board to the floor as Mac made the more intricate cuts around the heating pipes and the radiator, which we had opted to leave in place.

"Where have you been?" Mac demanded in that gruff voice that made tardy subcontractors quake in their steel-toed work boots.

"Digging up a bit of history," I said. "I was over at the historical society with Iver Jones."

"Maybe you could do something a bit more useful," Mac grumped. "Like produce our show."

He had a point. It wasn't every day that one caught a homeowner so obviously caught up in an old house project. I found Iggy and Kat out back having an extended smoke break. They grabbed their gear and strolled into the kitchen with the camera rolling. Chip was so intent on his work that he barely looked up. Iggy got a close up of him, then zoomed in on Mac, who was making a cardboard template of the tricky cut around the radiator pipe. In the background, the powerful whine of a siren began to build and we had to stop filming for a minute. Chesapeake City Volunteer Fire Company still summoned its firefighters with a siren that filled your skull with noise. The first time we had heard it, some of us thought it was an air raid siren and debated heading for the Cosden House cellar. We weren't the only ones startled by the siren. At one of the bed and breakfasts closer to the fire house, guests sometimes tumbled out of bed in a panic, thinking that a bomber squadron or some other cataclysm was bearing down upon them.

We had since learned that if the whistle blew once, an ambulance crew was needed. Three times and the firefighters were being summoned. Either something was burning or there was a car accident. As it turned out, the whistle wasn't really necessary because most of the firefighters and ambulance crew carried pagers that served the same purpose, or they could be texted on their mobile phones. But tradition died hard in a small town.

Once the whistle faded, Mac explained for the camera what he was doing about the radiator pipes. Making a cardboard template took the guesswork out of trying to cut the actual subfloor material to fit. Then Iggy panned around the bare walls and empty floor. All in all, it was good stuff. The video would be great to run alongside shots of the transformed kitchen. It felt as if *Delmarva Renovators* was getting back on track after the unsettling events of the last two days. I could almost forget that the star of our show continued to be absent. Jenny still hadn't called to let me know when she was coming back. Or that she wasn't.

Pushing that thought from my mind, I went in search of Marsha. I found her upstairs with Cindy Pritchard, picking out tiles for the bathroom. Marsha had lined up the tile choices on a shelf so that she and Cindy could look them over. I shouted down for Kat to bring up a camera so we could catch their discussion on vid. The lighting wasn't nearly so good up here in the bath, so Kat set up some lights. Cindy was a natural in front of the camera, but I made them have their discussion three times while Kat filmed.

"That was kind of fun," Cindy said, once we'd gotten a final take. "But it all looks so easy when I watch the show. It's hard trying to make some sense when you know people might actually be watching."

"You did fine," I told her. "You did better than me. There's a reason I stay back here behind the cameras, you know."

Cindy was starting to smile in that a star-is-born kind of way. I loved that look. It meant that the homeowners would keep writing checks to fund the show. "Do you know when this will be on?"

"In the next week or so. I'll be sure to let you know."

"My friends will want to watch."

Watch. I liked the sound of that, as if our show was actually on television instead of a Web cast. But you had to start somewhere. Today, the Internet. Tomorrow, late-night cable. Next thing you know, we'd be giving *This Old House* a run for its money.

There were several benefits to an online show. First, we didn't need a huge budget. We'd mainly gotten started using credit cards. Some of the cameras we were using were just a step above cell phone video. But that was okay; it worked online. We could interact with our audience through e-mails, blogs and comment posts. And by tracking our statistics, we got instant feedback on what worked and what didn't. That was how I knew that Jenny's absence was hurting us.

Back when I came up with the idea for *Delmarva Renovators*, most people had nodded and said encouraging things the way they do with most half-baked ideas, just to be polite. But when Mac and I actually went through with it, just about everyone thought we had lost our minds. They wondered why I couldn't just have a normal mid-life crisis and get myself a Porsche. You find out that your real friends are the ones who believe in your dreams right along with you—Mac, for one.

My sons thought it was cool and they had new respect for the old man. What they didn't know was that the show had yet to turn a profit. The kids were still of an age when they believed food appeared magically on the table and that the lights came on of their own accord. They didn't realize money made it all happen. I raided my 401(k) and borrowed heavily from our home equity. Kept driving my old truck. With Ellen, I talked up the benefits of a state university for our boys instead of private colleges. I guess I was beyond caring much about her opinion anyhow, sad to say. The boys were really all we had in common these days.

Launching the show's first real old house project had provided a good excuse to move out. In front of the boys, Ellen and I could pretend it was all for the show and not because mom and dad didn't love each other anymore.

Until *Delmarva Renovators* caught on, we would just have to keep things afloat on our credit cards. A big tool company or two might get interested in backing us someday. They could buy us new trucks with their logo on the doors—

Mac's voice rumbled up from below. "Hammer, the police are here again and they want to talk to you."

Those weren't words I wanted to hear, but I went downstairs to find DFC Maureen Sullivan in the foyer. She was all business. Her wide-brimmed hat was tucked under one arm while the thumb of her right hand was hooked through her black utility belt. The creases of her uniform pants looked sharp enough to cut you. A badge gleamed on her uniform blouse. And somehow she looked an inch or two taller as she held herself ramrod-stiff. But it was her eyes that I found most disturbing. They had gone hard as marbles as she looked me up and down.

"Mr. Martell, I have a few questions for you," she said. She broke off her gaze long enough to look around the room, which was beginning to get crowded. Mac wandered in from the kitchen, filling the doorway with his bulk. "We can speak someplace in private if you prefer."

"No secrets here," I said, wondering what had brought about the change in DFC Sullivan. She looked angry as a thunderstorm about to break.

"Were you at Franklin Hall earlier today?" she asked.

"Yes, I was at the town museum a couple of hours ago. Why?"

"Did you see Iver Jones while you were there?" DFC Sullivan asked.

"He was helping me do some research."

I noticed that Mac was looking at me with one eyebrow raised, which was his "I can't wait to hear this" expression. I hadn't bothered to tell him what I was up to or what I had found, so he was probably still unhappy that I'd left Chip Pritchard to help with the kitchen floor instead. He didn't have to tell me that we were supposed to be fixing up an old house, not solving a ninety-year-old mystery.

"Someone pushed Iver down the stairs."

"Good Lord," I said. "Is he all right?"

The deputy continued to study my face for a few seconds before answering. I caught on to the fact that she suspected I might have been the one to push Iver. DFC Sullivan's stare was sure making me feel guilty, even though I knew I was innocent. "An ambulance took him to the hospital," the deputy finally said, her eyes not leaving my face, though she did shift her stance enough to make her leather utility belt creak. "That's all we know right now."

"That would explain why the fire company whistle went off," Mac said.

DFC Sullivan wasn't finished with me yet. "Mr. Martell, you were the last person to be seen with him."

"You actually think I pushed Iver down the stairs?"

"It's him all right," Mac said gravely. "One time we were in line at a wedding buffet and he shoved me right out of the way to get the last of the canapés. Better put the handcuffs on him."

"You think this is funny?" Now DFC Sullivan had that

angry edge to her voice that really made her sound like a cop. "We might be talking about an attempted murder charge here."

"Iver Jones is a nosy old git," Mac growled back. He wasn't about to be intimidated by a deputy. "There's probably a dozen people in this town who wouldn't mind shoving him down the stairs. You better start making a list."

I could see that Mac had taken some of the wind out of the deputy's sails. She turned back to me and asked, "So what was Iver Jones helping you research?"

"It had to do with the brick," I said.

"What brick?"

"She doesn't know about the brick?" Mac said.

"Right after lunch today someone threw a brick through the front window," I explained. "I guess I didn't get around to reporting it to the police yet."

"Why not?" the deputy demanded.

"I wanted more information first, which was why I went down to the town museum and got Iver to help me do some research."

"About a brick?" DFC Sullivan sounded puzzled.

"There was a name scratched on the brick," I said. "Does the name Leo Cosden ring a bell?"

"I guess I'm not as up-to-date as you on my Cosden family history," the deputy said. "Bring me up to speed. Who was Leo?"

"Leo was Captain Ezra Cosden's older brother," I explained. "He was a successful Chesapeake Bay captain himself. More successful than his brother, by some accounts. He owned three ships that carried produce and lumber from Chesapeake City to Baltimore or Philadelphia. You might even say that Leo was on his way to becoming a wealthy man."

"Ah, but something must have happened to Leo," Mac said, filling in the blanks. "Mainly because we've never heard of him."

"A storm happened to him. A nor'easter that struck on October twentieth, nineteen-thirteen."

"Go on," the deputy said.

"Next to a hurricane, nor'easters are the worst storms there are in this part of the Chesapeake Bay," I said. "You get them in the fall or winter. Your blizzards around here are usually nor'easters, for instance. Leo Cosden knew a storm was coming. All the signs were there. But he was an experienced captain and maybe a bit daring. Maybe he was used to having luck on his side. How else had he acquired a fleet of three ships at a fairly young age? He must have thought he could outrun the storm. None of his crew would go with him, so he decided to sail the ship himself. The ship was small enough that he could do that, but not if he got caught in the middle of a nor'easter."

"Just a wild guess here," Mac said. "Leo didn't make it home."

"His ship went down near Poole's Island. The newspaper account said that his brother, Ezra, was worried and sailed out to look for him as soon as the storm started to let up. He found the wreckage. There was no sign of Leo Cosden."

Mac and Deputy Sullivan exchanged a look.

"When were you going to tell me about this?" Mac grumped.

I looked at Deputy Sullivan. "Tell me something, Deputy. Iver is getting up there in years. Are you sure he didn't fall down the stairs? This is important."

"I'm not sure how much I should tell you." Deputy Sullivan shifted from foot to foot. "When the ambulance crew was there, he came to long enough to tell them he was pushed."

"All right. If somebody shoved Iver down the stairs, I think that kind of proves my theory."

Deputy Sullivan crossed her arms on her chest. "And what theory is that?"

"Ezra Cosden inherited his missing brother's remaining ships. According to what Iver showed me, Ezra also happened to be building a house at the time."

"You mean this house?" Mac asked.

I nodded. "The channel where Leo's ship went down is fifty

feet deep in places," I said. "His body was never found. Until yesterday."

It took a moment for what I had just said to sink in.

"That's crazy," the deputy said.

"The brick through the window was a pretty obvious clue," I pointed out. "Someone wanted to make sure we knew whose body was inside the wall of the house."

"So what you're saying is that Leo Cosden didn't drown in the storm," she said.

"Whoever threw the brick through the window doesn't think he did."

Deputy Sullivan eyed me skeptically. "This is a lot to swallow," she said.

"What we have here is a ninety-some-year-old murder."

"I'm more concerned about what happened about ninety-some minutes ago when someone pushed an old man down the stairs," she said.

"Someone wasn't happy that Iver was helping me," I said. "If this is a Cosden family secret going back nine decades, you've got a lot of suspects."

"Okay, I'm making a list," the deputy said. "Hmm. Let me think. Right now, you're still at the top of it. In fact, you're the only one on it."

"Are you going to arrest him now?" Mac asked. "If you are, I'd better get busy baking a cake with a file in it. Or maybe a hacksaw. That would work better."

"I'm not arresting him yet," she said, her steely eyes on me. "Not yet. But for your sake, Mr. Martell, I hope Iver Jones pulls through, or you might be looking at a second-degree homicide charge. In the meantime, don't even think about leaving the county."

CHAPTER 8

At dusk I sent everyone home. Mac stayed behind, finishing up in the upstairs bath, where he was framing in a linen closet that Cindy Pritchard had insisted on at the last minute. I could hear him banging around and grumbling to himself. He was sore at me for not telling him sooner about Leo Cosden. But I had wanted to get a few things straight before I shared any half-baked theories, even with Mac. For starters, I wanted to know more about Leo Cosden—but with Iver Jones in the hospital, that wasn't likely. Whoever had pushed him down the stairs knew just what they were doing.

I wondered who had reported seeing me at the town museum around the same time as Iver's accident. It could have been one of half a dozen people who had seen me coming and going at Franklin Hall.

I wandered into the kitchen and started cleaning up. Something clattered outside. "Who's there?"

Beyond the back door, darkness gathered. The view of the canal, normally so breathtaking, now made the back yard feel lonely and windswept. Spring was coming, but it still looked wintry out there.

I told myself the noise was only a dog nosing around, but thinking of the orderly pile of paving bricks and salvaged lumber outside it seemed unlikely these would hold much interest for a stray. Everybody was gone except for Mac and he was bumping around upstairs somewhere. Maybe it was the gathering gloom, but the thought occurred to me that perhaps Mac wasn't the one causing the noises overhead. The floor joists seemed to pop and groan of their own accord. Considering that it had harbored a body until yesterday, the Cosden House had every right to be haunted. I listened for a moment, but hearing nothing further, I started coiling an electrical cord.

We had work lights set up in the kitchen, but throughout the rest of the house many of the light circuits were off or disconnected so that shadows filled the other rooms. The Cosden House had been built soon after electric power came to this corner of Maryland; just a few years before, oil lamps and candles would have been the only means to dispel the darkness. Tonight, it was as if the nineteenth century had returned to the Cosden House. A dusky twilight flowed like liquid into the corners, creating pools of shadow.

Looking around, I was overwhelmed by how much there was to do. And the list seemed to get longer all the time. I felt like that donkey with the carrot dangling on a stick in front of him, forever out of reach as he pulled his cart along.

Old houses are never really finished. There's always one more repair to tackle, big or small, and it usually involves paint, caulk, joint compound and a few artfully placed nails or screws. Every old house takes on a personality of its own and each has its own unique problems. If you've ever taken on an old house project, you'll know what I mean. You'll never need a hobby.

I had worked on my share of old houses over the years. The first house my wife and I owned was half of a city duplex. A good, solid house with three bedrooms above a living room, dining room and kitchen. We were barely more than kids ourselves back then and fixing up an old house together felt romantic. We made a point of making love in every one of those rooms—even on the stairs. In between, we also stripped wallpaper, rewired, insulated, painted, re-roofed and basically turned our old house into a new one—only to find ourselves forced to sell and move because of a career opportunity in another city.

The next house we owned was a split level, a real seventies horror. It was the kind of low-maintenance home you moved into when you were working some job fifty and sixty hours a week. I guess it says something that the only projects we took on there involved painting and carpeting, although I did refinish the basement living room. Hardly our dream home. More of a stopping point on the way to somewhere else. We had our babies in that house. And our first serious arguments followed by chilly silences. I see now that those houses were learning projects for a renovator, like unpublished novels are for a writer.

Our old Victorian came next. In some strange way, I think Ellen and I had thought the house might get us through our own rough patch by giving us something to work on together. The house remained a work in progress—which is to say I hadn't done much of anything. It was where our sons were growing up and where my wife and I had grown apart.

I moved around the Cosdens' kitchen, attacking piles of sawdust with a broom. Mac and I often stayed late to get things ready for the next day. Spending time in the mornings sweeping up the previous day's mess or hunting for tools was like starting off the day with your boots on the wrong feet.

The back steps creaked. The noise made the hairs on the back of my neck turn to steel bristles.

"Mac, is that you? Quit fooling around." But I was pretty sure it wasn't Mac. He would have had to go out the front door without me hearing and then walk all the way around to the back steps.

I couldn't see beyond the black pane of glass, but I knew that somebody was watching me from the darkness. Don't ask me how I could tell. It's one of those instincts left over from when our ancestors stared into the night beyond the mouth of the cave.

There was no functioning porch light to turn on. Quickly, I reached up and angled the work light toward the back door.

The harsh glare lit up the pale face of Rory Cosden. He had been standing in the darkness on the back steps, just out of sight.

"Rory?" I hoped the back door muffled the shrillness of my voice. My heart pounded.

"You scared the hell out of me."

He took a step closer and I reached to open the door. Rory stepped inside without uttering a word.

The unfinished kitchen instantly grew smaller. Rory Cosden was not a tall man, but he was built square as a cinderblock. Beneath a shock of unruly black hair, his face was the color of dough. Above the fresh scent of new lumber I could smell him. Alcohol and a goatish scent as if he hadn't showered in a while. I doubted that Rory's drink of choice was beer or even off-the-shelf whiskey. Some of the Cosden clan members were still known for making moonshine in the woods around here. White lightning. From the look in Rory's eyes I guessed that a little madness was cooked in with the mash.

"What can I do for you, Rory?" I asked. "Did you want to see how we're coming along with the house?"

"Leave my family alone," he said, shoving his fists deeper into the pockets of his denim coat, the kind with a collar made of acrylic sheepskin.

So much for small talk. "I don't understand," I said. "All we're trying to do is bring some life back to your great-grand-father's house. We'll make it as good as it was, maybe even better."

"I ain't talkin' about the house," Rory said, slurring his words. "Just leave my family be, you and the rest of your people."

"But we haven't done anything to your family!"

"Then what do you call going over to the historical society and digging up them old newspapers, huh? You're dragging things out into the light that's better left alone."

"This is crazy, Rory. I'm only trying to find things out that have to do with the house. There can't be anything wrong with that."

But I could see that Rory wasn't listening. He swayed as if some gale I couldn't detect was blowing through the kitchen. He kept nodding his head like he was agreeing with something somebody other than me was saying.

I'm a little slow sometimes, but I was beginning to get a clear picture of what was going on. *Someone* had pushed Iver Jones down the steps at the historical society. Since I knew that particular someone hadn't been me, I was pretty sure now that it must have been Rory Cosden. If he had tried to silence Iver, maybe I was next on his list.

Flicking my eyes around the empty room, I tried to find something I could use to defend myself if Rory turned violent. I'd been in the middle of sweeping up, but doubted I could beat Rory senseless with a broom. I was a little taller than him, but he outweighed me by fifty pounds and he was a good deal younger—plus I've never been much of a brawler. What I needed was a weapon. I spotted a hefty length of two-by-four near the empty space where the refrigerator would go and started inching toward it.

"You don't get it," Rory said. "You come into this town, you stir things up, and then you think you can just walk away from it all when you're done. Well, that ain't what's gonna happen."

"What's so bad about the past, Rory? What don't you want me to know?"

"You already know too much," he nearly shouted.

"Calm down."

"Don't tell me what to do," Rory said. One of his big fists emerged from the pocket of his denim jacket. I chanced taking an entire step toward the two-by-four, but what I saw next stopped me in my tracks. Rory was holding a folding knife in his fist. He flicked it open so I could see the short, curved blade. It flashed in the light. I recognized it as what deer hunters called a skinning knife. Not especially big, but wickedly sharp.

"Whoa," I said. "Rory, it doesn't have to be this way."

"I'm going to shut your mouth for good."

I heard a noise behind me and turned to see Mac walk in and grab the two-by-four I'd been eying. I would have needed two hands to get a good grip, but he held it in one fist as easily as I had gripped the broom handle.

"Rory, what the hell are you doing?" he demanded. "Put the knife down.

Rory took his wild eyes off me and studied Mac as if figuring his chances. He tucked his chin down like a bull getting ready to charge.

Mac hefted the two-by-four in two hands this time, like a baseball bat. "Rory," he growled.

Rory hesitated, then dropped the knife to his side. Even drunk and angry, he must have seen that Mac would knock his head over the back fence before he could get close enough with the knife.

"This ain't over," Rory said, turning his gaze back to me. "There's gonna be trouble as long as you keep digging around asking questions."

"Go home, Rory," Mac said, the two-by-four resting now on his shoulder. He sounded every bit like the cop he used to be. "Go home and sleep it off."

Without another word, Rory turned and went back out into the night. He slammed the door behind him so hard that the whole house shook.

"It's about time you showed up," I said, walking over to the back door and locking it in case Rory changed his mind.

"You never were much good in a fight," Mac said. "One of these days I'm not going to be around to save your sorry ass. What was that all about, anyhow?"

"You heard him," I said. "Rory wants me to stop digging up the past."

"You mean like Leo Cosden? Rory's nuts. That's ancient history."

"Maybe not if you're a Cosden," I pointed out.

Mac tossed the two-by-four into a corner. "Did you get a look at that knife? I think we just figured out who slashed our tires out in front of the Bohemia Café this morning."

"I've also got a pretty good idea of who shoved Iver Jones down the stairs at the historical society," I added.

"Rory?"

"He knew I was over there talking to Iver about the Cosdens."

Mac nodded. "That makes him a likely candidate. It's also a good bet that he told the police you were at the town museum. I can't think of a better way to point the finger at someone else. And believe me, when it comes to police work most cops are like electricity. They look for the path of least resistance."

Mac had a good point. If Rory got their attention focused on me, the police wouldn't have gone looking for anybody else.

"I'd like to stop by the hospital and talk to Iver," I said.

"The police won't like that. You're still a suspect as far as they're concerned, so you'd better stay away from Iver."

"Okay. Maybe you should talk to him. You're the ex-cop."

"A big lug like me? I dunno. The nurse will take one look at me and call security. Besides, that old man never liked me much." Mac looked thoughtful. "Let's see if Marsha will talk to him instead. Marsha is so nice and ladylike. She could sweet talk the tusks off an elephant. She'll make short work of those nurses."

"Good idea," I agreed. "Listen, Mac, I'm sorry I didn't tell you sooner about Leo Cosden. I just wanted to work it out in my head before I started sharing a bunch of crazy theories with everyone."

"I think Rory just proved your theories," he said. Mac smirked. "And if he'd had his way, they would have died with you, too."

So Rory had vandalized our vehicles, maybe even pushed an old man down the stairs. All because we were delving into the Cosden family's past. The question was, who had hurled the brick with Leo Cosden's name scratched into it through the front window? Rory wanted us to leave the past alone, but somebody out there was trying just as hard to make sure the past wasn't forgotten.

CHAPTER 9

When things aren't going your way, I'm a firm believer in drowning one's sorrows in beer and pizza. So that's exactly what Mac and I did at a pizza place in the county seat. After our run-in with Rory Cosden, we needed some serious comfort food, and the restaurant was far enough from Chesapeake City that we could be anonymous faces in the crowd. We ordered a pitcher of Yuengling lager and a large pizza with the works. The rest of the world—and our arteries—be damned.

Mac also must have been thinking over what happened back at the house. He ate without saying a word, an unusual occurrence for Mac, so I could tell something was weighing on his mind. Finally, he slammed down his beer and tossed aside the crust, or what he liked to call the "pizza bones." "Hammer, what the hell have we gotten ourselves into?" he asked. "We're supposed to fix up old houses for an online renovation show, not solve mysteries and almost get ourselves knifed in the process."

"What I can't figure is that Rory seemed all right whenever he stopped by the house. Maybe a little soft in the head from in-breeding or whatever. But if he comes around again I can see there's just going to be trouble." I reached for another slice and sprinkled it liberally with garlic, oregano and hot pepper. "We could call the police and get him locked up for assault or something."

Mac shrugged. "One of his cousins would just bail him out in the morning and we'd be right back where we started, only with the whole Cosden clan mad at us."

"Somehow, I don't think we've heard the last of Rory." The image of him waving a deer-skinning knife at me was hard to forget. The more I thought about it, the angrier I got. Mac was right. What had we gotten ourselves into? "I hate to say it, but I don't think we'll be able to finish the house until we figure out what this is all about."

"So what is this all about?"

I sighed. "I wish I knew, Mac. A body in the wall, tires slashed, a brick through the window, an old man shoved down the stairs, a knife waved in our faces. You'd think we had enough trouble as it is trying to figure out how to get that old clawfoot tub out of the second-floor bathroom."

"Been there, done that." Mac groaned. "I'd rather wrestle an alligator down the stairs."

I had to smile. The bathtub incident had made for an interesting episode. At first, Cindy Pritchard had been charmed by the original tub and we started renovating the bathroom around it. A segment on reglazing the old tub would have been interesting—but we never got that far. Last week, she had fallen out of love and decided on a more modern walk-in shower. The claw-foot monstrosity had to go. Mac wasn't kidding when he compared wrestling an alligator to maneuvering a bulky cast iron tub that weighed several hundred pounds out the bathroom door, through the hallway and down the staircase without damaging the old woodwork and newell post. Actually, I thought it was more like wrestling a greased pig through a china shop. Now Cindy was making noises about putting the claw-foot tub back. My plan was to haul it as far away as possible before she could change her mind. Like maybe putting it on the next scrap boat to China.

Mac grabbed another slice with all the gusto of a grizzly snatching a salmon out of a mountain stream. "I hate to say this, but I'm almost tempted to give up on the house and walk away."

I jabbed my slice of 'za at him. "Don't even start thinking like that. Don't psych yourself out. We can't afford it."

"I know that, Hammer. But there's always a breaking point in any renovation." He swigged his beer. "All that dust gets me down."

"One day at a time, Mac. Every day gets us closer to the goal."

"It would go better if we had more help."

I knew he was talking about Jenny. There was still no word from our AWOL carpenter. "We'll just have to do the best we can."

"I can't believe she would bail on us without any explanation," Mac said. "It's not like Jenny at all. She really left us in the lurch."

I glanced at Mac, a confession on the tip of my tongue. Should I tell him what happened? I guess it bothered me that he was blaming Jenny when it was more my fault than hers. Mac would find out the truth eventually, and he might be even more angry then that I hadn't told him sooner.

I cleared my throat. "You know, Mac, about Jenny . . . can I tell you something confidential?"

"What is it?" Worry lines creased his brow. "Is she in some kind of trouble?"

"Nothing like that. But she left the show for a reason, and I'm pretty sure that reason was me."

Mac stared. "What are you talking about?"

"I don't want you to think this is kiss and tell. It's not like that. I just want you to understand why she left—so you don't blame her. That doesn't seem fair."

Realization swept over his face like a coat of fresh paint rolled on a blank wall. "Jesus. You slept with her."

"It was an accident—"

"You've got to be kidding. Banging your thumb is an accident. Banging Jenny is something else altogether. I can't believe this. *You had sex with Jenny.*" Mac's angry voice caused other diners to stare. They looked away when he slammed his fist on the table. The pizza platter and silverware clattered. "This is just—" He shook his head, at a loss for words.

"You know I feel bad about it. I'm not supposed to be sleeping with the crew."

"The *crew*? This is Jenny we're talking about." Mac stood so abruptly that his chair fell over. "You are such an asshole."

And then he walked out.

He also left behind a slice of pizza and half a pitcher of beer, so I knew this was serious.

I really hadn't expected Mac to leave me stranded, but after I paid the check and headed out to the parking lot, I discovered that the truck was gone. The night was dark except for a flickering street light and the shopping center was mostly deserted. Our hotel was on the other side of town. This must have been how the people who got left behind at Saigon felt.

Mac's reaction puzzled me. It was extreme, even for a guy given to throwing things in fits of rage. While I hadn't exactly thought he would slap me on the back and say *atta boy*, I hadn't expected him to get so upset. This wasn't about jeopardizing the show. With a sinking feeling, I realized that there was another possibility. Mac was jealous.

Mac and I went back a long way. Together, we had figured out how to be adults. He would give me a kidney if I needed one, and I would have given him one of mine. At the same time, we traded insults like they were baseball cards. Earlier tonight he had kept me from getting carved up by a moonshine-crazed Cosden. But I had just crossed some kind of line with Mac.

In the unwritten Code of Buddyhood, the absolute worst violation was to steal your best friend's girl. But in my defense, how could I steal her when he hadn't said anything about Jenny? You've got to have a lot of talents to fix up an old house, but so far, mind-reading wasn't one of them.

A more immediate problem was that our motel was several

miles away and it was getting late. I didn't particularly relish the thought of hiking across town, so I dragged out my cell phone and called Marsha for a ride. Ten minutes later her Saab pulled up out front.

"I thought you had your truck," she said.

"Mac had some errands to run, so I let him borrow it." I wasn't about to make more than one public confession tonight.

"I just left the hospital," Marsha said.

"Did you talk to Iver?"

"Yes, and you're off the hook," Marsha said. "Unless you happened to be wearing a wig and a pink sweatshirt this afternoon."

"What in the world are you talking about?"

"Iver told the sheriff's deputy that a woman with shoulder-length brown hair pushed him down the steps. She caught him off balance. And that his attacker was wearing a pink sweatshirt. Iver said that someone switched off the lights, so he didn't get a look at the woman's face."

"I do have that pink sweater that my wife bought me for Christmas two years ago," I pointed out.

"No wonder you're separated," Marsha said.

"Is Iver sure he didn't know who pushed him?"

"He said it all happened too fast."

"It's good to know I'm not going to jail."

"Not yet," Marsha said, giving me a sharp look. "But tell me whose bright idea it was to post the video of us finding the body?"

"It's our site," I said defensively. "We can do what we want."

"You just tell that to the police, Sugar. They've already been to the motel looking for you." At the next red light, Marsha reached into the back seat and then offered me a tub of store-bought brownies. "Brownie? Might as well. It could be your last one for a while if they lock you up."

There was no sign of Mac back at the hotel. I said good night to Marsha and spent a couple of hours updating our project blog. This was the place where I wrote about the things that didn't make it into the video version of events at the project house. I got onto the topic of how we hadn't known what to do with some of the light fixtures and ceiling fans we had ripped out of the house. It's a common problem in reno-vation—you rip out the old stuff but it's too good to throw in the Dumpster. Plus there's no point in taking up valuable Dumpster space—disposal service is not cheap—and was sending reusable items to the landfill really an environmentally responsible thing to do? As a kind of half measure, we had begun piling salvageable items in a shed on the property. So far, we had the light fixtures and fans, along with bathroom mirrors, a 1950s enamel sink, a refrigerator that more or less worked, plus a collection of lumber salvaged from the house.

We hadn't given much thought to these items other than to save them, but at some point I knew we would have to dispose of them before we tackled fixing up the shed—which was somewhere near the bottom of the project list. Marsha had suggested holding a sort of yard sale—but with the volatile atmosphere in town I wasn't so keen on that idea anymore (though I steered away from that particular topic in the blog). A bit of research turned up a Habitat for Humanity warehouse in Delaware that took donated items—everything from second-hand appliances to reusable building materials. The organization then used the warehouse as a kind of hardware store for its own projects, but was also open to the public. Funds from the sale of donated items went to help fund Habitat projects. I blogged for a bit about all of that. If we ever found time in our schedule, I was thinking that the warehouse would make a good field trip.

I was too tired to do much else with the site—sometimes I spent time trolling through the site in much the way a farmer walks his fields, just to see how things were going and what sort of comments we were getting. I tweaked the site in the same way that a farmer pulls a few weeds or mends a fence.

But tonight I felt bone weary. My boys were online, so I spent a few minutes messaging them. Zach had a math test in the morning. Charlie was opposed to soccer practice at the moment, so we went back and forth about that. He had made the commitment to play, I reminded him, so he had to stick with it. Finally, I closed up the laptop just as somebody knocked.

Actually, knocked was too polite a term. Somebody was pounding on the door. And they pounded harder when I didn't answer right away. I was pretty sure it wasn't Mac because the door hadn't gone flying off its hinges.

A couple of thoughts went through my mind. Was it Rory, coming back to finish what he started? Or maybe the police, as Marsha had warned, unhappy about the video we had posted.

I opened the door to find Iggy waiting on the other side, clutching his own laptop. In a way I was relieved it wasn't Mac, but I was also a little disappointed. I couldn't remember Mac ever being so angry with me, and I was hoping that would blow over sooner rather than later.

Iggy didn't wait for an invitation but came stalking into the room on his long legs.

"Have you seen it?" he demanded, his eyes backlit with exitement. That in itself was somewhat disturbing because Iggy was normally so nonchalant. This was a guy who didn't get rattled about spiders in a crawl space or even swarms of bats in an attic, but he was hanging onto his laptop now like a street corner preacher clutches a Bible.

"Seen what?"

"Our video, man! It's everywhere!"

It took me a moment to register what video Iggy was talking about. Then Iggy plunked down his computer and started pointing at the screen. "The number one clip on YouTube right now is ours! And if you Google us, man, we're all over the Web. How awesome is that!"

Iggy navigated the Web long enough to show me that the video of the mummified body tumbling out of the wall was getting its fifteen minutes of virtual fame. I felt a little sheepish being so oblivious to what was going on in cyberspace when our show was involved.

"You know what this means?" Iggy was practically shouting. "It means we're famous!"

I stared at the screen filled with site statistics in a state of disbelief. The number of hits had gone from an average of four thousand per day to more than forty thousand. We were famous, all right.

"Man, this is what we've been waiting for!" Iggy said as he peered over my shoulder.

He was right about that. Our website was getting the kind of hits—or should I say "unique visitors"—that we so desperately craved. Hits meant sponsors would finally notice us. But I couldn't escape the nagging thought that sometimes you have to be careful what you wish for.

CHAPTER 10

My pickup truck—with Mac in the passenger seat—had reappeared sometime during the night.

"Good morning," I said as I slid behind the wheel.

Mac grunted a reply, big arms crossed on his chest. He was wearing a fresh T-shirt, one that said, "I'd like to double your entendre," so I knew he must have returned to his room at some point. He didn't offer any explanation about where he'd been most of the night, and I didn't ask. A grunt was enough. We could work up to actual words later. I gave him a quick update about Iver Jones, but the ride down to Chesapeake City was otherwise quiet except for an overly cheerful DJ going on about traffic. But that was for the commute into Wilmington, Delaware. There wasn't much in the way of traffic congestion on the road into town, although we did get stuck behind a tractor at one point.

Old houses take on personalities of their own, and the Captain Cosden House was no exception. The place had seen more than ninety summers and winters, which tends to lend a certain *gravitas*. Maybe it was only my imagination, but I had the distinct feeling that the antique four-square house was glad to see us as we drove up.

"At least nobody burned it down during the night," grumped Mac. "After that brick through the window, I wasn't sure what to expect."

I took comfort in the fact that Mac was talking, even if he didn't sound all that happy.

We weren't the only early birds at the site. A sheriff's office vehicle pulled in behind us.

"I thought you were off the hook with that Iver business," Mac said, his eyes in our rear-view mirror.

"I have a feeling this is more about the video we posted of the body being found," I said. "If I get arrested, any chance you might bail me out?"

Mac seemed to think it over, so I could tell he hadn't gotten over my confession last night. "We have to talk later," he said.

"Okay, I just hope it's not down at the county jail."

Slowly, I got out of the truck, wondering if we were ever going to be left alone long enough to make some progress on the house. Deputy First Class Sullivan got out of the patrol car wearing mirrored sunglasses, which I did not take to be a good sign.

"We need to talk," she said, her tone of voice all business.

"I've been hearing that a lot this morning. Let's go inside," I suggested. "I can show you some of the work we've done in the last few days. I could even rustle up a cup of coffee."

"All right. But this isn't exactly a social call."

The deputy greeted Mac with a curt nod, but then Mac headed for the van and started pulling out tools, leaving the two of us to climb the steps to the front door. Inside, the empty house echoed with every footstep and the air smelled of drying spackle and dust. I went straight for the kitchen to brew a pot of coffee. Although the room was still down to bare studs and loose wires hung from the ceiling, we had rigged a coffee station to keep us going. The coffee sometimes came out gritty with plaster sand or with flecks of sawdust floating in it—but it was better than running to the Bohemia Café or even The Hole in the Wall every time we needed a caffeine fix, which was pretty often. Besides, with the way things were in town right now, I wasn't so sure I wanted to spend any more time in the Bohemia Café than necessary. I wasn't so worried about running into Rory again, but I didn't want to field nosy questions or, worse yet, experience the expectant hush fall over the diner when I walked in.

"You've made progress," Deputy Sullivan said.

"I'm glad you think so. Right now it feels like we're swimming against the current."

While the coffee brewed, I tried to delay the tongue lashing I felt sure was coming from the deputy by poking my head into the dining room, where Mac was getting ready to start replacing the sash weights for the dining room windows. Iggy and Kat were setting up to film Mac at work. They had the high-def camera out and the room was blazing with studio lights. Electrical cords snaked across the dusty floorboards.

"Please don't trip over anything," Iggy warned. "We're down to our last working set of lights."

"Filming an old house project is a little rough on the equipment," I explained to the deputy. "Dust gets into everything. Things get knocked over."

"And bodies fall out of walls," Mac added. "It's also rough on the crew. We don't have stunt doubles."

Deputy Sullivan looked around at the equipment, but didn't comment. She seemed to be more interested in the sash weight Mac was holding.

"My house doesn't even have those," she said. "I have to use a stick to keep the old windows open. The main part of the house is a log cabin, so they never bothered with that kind of thing."

"This was high-tech in nineteen thirteen," I said.

Modern windows slide on a vinyl track and friction holds them in place when opened. Our old windows relied on a system that used a metal pulley about the size of a silver dollar at the top of each side of the window sash. The wall space on either side of the window frame was hollow. A removable wooden hatch gave access to the hidden pocket. The space was designed so that an elongated weight made of pig iron dangled inside. The weight was designed much like a fishing sinker, with a hole at the top to which was attached cotton clothesline cord. The cord ran inside the wall from the weight to a pulley at the top of the window frame, where it emerged and ran down the window into a groove on the inside of the lower sash. The end of the cord was knotted and a nail driven through the knot secured it inside a small hole on the side of the sash. Then, as the sash was raised or lowered, the weight inside the wall served as a counterweight to hold it in place—without a stick.

"Pretty cool system." DFC Sullivan peered through the access hatch at the darkness inside the wall. "Any more bodies hiding in there?"

"Very funny," I said.

"That coffee ready yet?"

We left Mac to work on the sash weights and headed for the kitchen. I grabbed an empty mug and handed it to the deputy while I reached for the coffee pot.

Deputy Sullivan just stood there, staring into the mug I had given her.

"What's wrong?" I asked.

She upended the mug and a shapeless furry thing fluttered to the floor. I had seen enough of them around old houses to realize that Deputy Sullivan's coffee mug had been the final resting place for a dead bat.

"I hope that wasn't your sick idea of a practical joke," she said. "I'm really not in the mood."

"What, you don't take bats in your coffee? Sorry about that." I handed her a clean mug. "Guaranteed sterile, if you don't count sawdust. How 'bout cream and sugar?"

"I think I'll stick with bat—I mean, *black*," she said.

Stepping around the bat's remains, I poured two coffees. There really wasn't anywhere to sit in the kitchen, so we went out on the back porch and settled ourselves on a couple of folding lawn chairs. The weather was turning nice—it was one of those soft May mornings—but the house itself had not yet shaken off its winter chill. The cold and damp had seeped deep into the timbers and walls.

"I think you know why I'm here this morning," she said. "You posted that video online in complete disregard to what you were asked to do."

"Nobody asked me to do or not do anything," I pointed out. "The sheriff's office took the video for evidence. We happened to have a copy."

"We confiscated the video to keep it from ending up on your website."

"That was never stated directly," I said. "It's our video. It's our show. We did with it what we thought was best."

"What, are you a lawyer now, too? I'd stick with old houses if I were you—it looks like you've got all you can handle in that department, anyhow."

I felt myself redden and would have said something harsh in reply if I hadn't noticed the faintest of smiles playing over Deputy Sullivan's lips. Then she took a sip and made a face. "Gritty."

"Plaster sand," I said. "It gets into everything."

Deputy Sullivan wasn't ready to let me off the hook just yet. She waggled the cup of coffee at me like a billy club. "What if the victim has family out there? How do you think they would feel?"

"Considering that the victim has been dead for at least ninety years, somehow I don't think he's fresh in anyone's mind."

"You had no business posting that video online," she said stubbornly.

Two could play at that game. "It's our video," I pointed out. "It's our show. We can do what we want."

"One word from me to the sheriff and he'll get the county to yank your building permit. You'll have a show, but you won't have a house to work on."

"That sounds like a threat."

"Consider it a warning to behave yourself from now on."

At least she hadn't said anything about taking the video off our website. Not that it would have made much difference. The video was floating around out there in cyberspace. You couldn't take something like that back. The genie was out of the bottle.

I decided to change the subject before Deputy Sullivan took out her handcuffs. "I've been wondering. Why would Leo Cosden be entombed in his brother's house?"

"That's the million dollar question, isn't it?"

"One of my crew pointed out that this whole body-in-the-wall scenario is a little like the Edgar Allan Poe story, *The Cask of Amontillado*. I read it back in high school. There's an Italian aristocrat, Montressor, who believes he has been insulted by his friend, Fortunato. So one night when Fortunato is deep in his cups, Montressor lures him into the cellar under his mansion with the promise of tasting a rare wine stored there. Then he chains the drunken Fortunato inside a little chamber, and walls him in. Fortunato wails 'For the love of God, Montresor!' and Montresor replies, 'Yes, for the love of God!' It's a story of revenge, but the reader can only think that whatever Fortunato has done doesn't justify such a horrible murder. But it does, you see, in Montressor's mind, because it's the mind of a madman."

Deputy Sullivan nodded. "So what you're saying is that there might not be a rational explanation for why Captain Ezra Cosden would put his brother's body in the wall of his new house." She sighed. "Why do I have the feeling that this is all going to get a whole lot uglier?"

"There's nothing messier than a family feud," I said. "Even one from 1913."

Deputy Sullivan was just about to chance another sip from her coffee mug when there came a terrific scream from the kitchen behind us. It sounded like Marsha. The deputy started for the doorway, one hand on the holster of her pistol.

I stopped her before she went rushing through the house with gun drawn. "It's okay," I said. "I think our design consultant just found that dead bat."

Sure enough, Marsha came bounding out a moment later. "There's a vampire bat," she sputtered. "In the kitchen."

"Don't worry," I said. "I'll sprinkle some garlic on it later."

Marsha gave me a withering look. "Not funny." She walked around the entire house and went in the front door rather than pass through the kitchen again.

Deputy Sullivan shook her head and handed me the empty coffee mug. "Just try to stay out of trouble, okay? Seems to me you've got your hands full here without trying to solve any long-ago murders."

We walked back out to her patrol car, chatting about nothing in particular, and I watched her drive off. Truth be told, people with badges and guns generally made me nervous, but Deputy Sullivan was giving me that vibe that said *I'm free Saturday night*. I'd have to think about that. If I was misreading things, the last thing I wanted to do was make a fool of us both.

Mac came out on the front porch and glanced at the empty coffee mugs in my hand. There was a reddish-pink stain on the rim of Deputy Sullivan's coffee mug.

"Huh," Mac said. "It's not every cop who wears lipstick on the job."

He ought to know, having been one. "Is that unusual?"

"Not unless you're trying to make a good impression."

I dumped the mugs in the kitchen and went out back to work on repairing some of the windows. While replacing the sash weights, Mac had found a few more windows that needed help. It might have been better to replace all the old windows in the house, but that wasn't really an option, even given the substantial budget provided by the owners. New, historically accurate and energy efficient replacements for the Cosden House would have cost as much as one thousand dollars per window. Simply replacing the windows with wooden Pella or Marvin units would likely not have been approved by the town's historical commission. The problem was that each and every window in the old captain's house was unique. Each upper sash was divided into fifteen individual panes or "lights" in an arts and crafts style. Replicating that exact window style with custom-made replacements was simply too time-consuming and expensive. The cost of a custom, wood-clad window with multiple "lights" was prohibitive, even for the king and queen of doggy doo. So we repaired the old windows instead. It took a lot of time and elbow grease—though it made for some good video—and it saved the Pritchards a bundle. It was a fact I had pointed out to them repeatedly in an effort to cover up our other foibles.

Repairing each window was a lot of work. Some of the panes were cracked and required replacement. The old glazing crumbled at the slightest touch. I had set up a makeshift workbench beneath an overhang of the shed out back. Long ago, someone might have parked a Model T or even a buggy there. The shed was filled to the rafters with all those items we weren't quite sure what to do with—too good for the Dumpster, not quite good enough to go back in the house.

I grabbed a fresh project window and laid it across a pair of sawhorses. We had already filmed this enough times that I didn't feel compelled to drag Iggy or Kat over with one of the digital cameras. Besides, they were busy with Mac and his sash weights at the moment.

The glazing came in a big metal can that I pried open with a screwdriver. A screwdriver and a glazing tool—which kind of resembled a tiny spatula with notches and sharper edges—were all you really needed to do this job. All the old compound had already been scraped away, so I got a new pane of glass from the custom-made stack I'd ordered at the hardware store. The pane fit tightly in the window frame, and I used glazing points—small galvanized triangles—to hold the pane in place, using the screwdriver to press them into the wood. Next, I painted the wood with linseed oil. I used the glazing tool to dig a glop of compound out of the can, then rolled it between my palms. The heat from the friction made the compound softer and more pliable. I kept rolling until the compound had been transformed into a shape about the length and thickness of a pencil. That was laid along the seam between the wood and glass, covering the glazing points. I used the spatula edge of the glazing tool to press the compound into a neat seam, and then used the notched edge to create corners. The linseed oil helped the compound bond to the old wood, which would have sucked out all the moisture otherwise. I kept going, pane by pane, until the window looked good as new. I tried not to think about the fact that there were several dozen more to go.

I was just setting aside the window when Marsha came down the back steps and stalked purposefully toward me. "There you are," she said. "I wondered where you were hiding."

"I'm not hiding," I said. "I'm working. Grab a window. I'll show you how it's done."

"Not in my job description." Marsha flipped her scarf around her neck with such force that I felt a breeze. "Where I come from, people don't leave dead bats on the floor. They have the decency to clean them up."

"I was in the middle of being browbeaten by a sheriff's deputy," I said. "Guess I forgot."

"Uh huh. Browbeaten? From the way you act around that deputy, I think you wouldn't mind if she took you in for a little extra interrogation."

"Let's just say she can spank me with a rubber hose anytime she wants."

"I always knew you were ahead of your time, Tom, but you're turning into a dirty old man a few decades early." Marsha bit back a laugh, not quite ready to forgive me. "That pretty deputy can keep her damn rubber hoses. If I find you leaving any more bats lying around I'm going to beat you with a shovel."

At that moment, there was a shrill scream from the direction of the house. Kat. Marsha and I exchanged a look. She hadn't picked up the bat, either.

I folded my arms across my chest and raised my eyebrows.

"You were saying?"

"Never mind."

I turned back to the stack of old windows and was just getting ready to put another victim up on the sawhorses when Marsha said in an urgent tone, "Tom, you better have a look at this."

Quickly, I turned around and followed her stare. A battered white pickup truck rolled slowly through the unpaved gravel alley behind the house. The man behind the wheel was none other than Rory Cosden. I had given Marsha and the rest of the crew a heads up that Rory was bad news. I looked around for some kind of weapon, the incident from the night before still fresh in my mind. The only thing handy was the flathead screwdriver. I picked it up and stuck it in my back pocket, figuring it was better than nothing. Rory came to a stop no more than thirty feet away, glared at us, and then drove off so fast that his spinning tires spat gravel.

"That guy is giving me the creeps," Marsha said. "What was that all about?"

"I'm not sure." I put down the screwdriver, glad I hadn't needed it as a weapon. It was puny compared to Rory's skinning knife. What was I going to do with a screwdriver, poke him in the eye? "If you see him around here again, call the police."

CHAPTER 11

Sometime after lunch, Mac's chilly silence started getting annoying, and I felt like I needed to escape the Cosden House for a while. Neither the police nor Rory Cosden had shown up in a couple of hours, so it seemed safe to get away.

I hopped in my truck and drove over to see Pete Morrison. I had a business proposition for him. Pete's cottage and studio were perched on a high shelf of land that overlooked Back Creek and the tidal marsh that formed the eastern boundary of the town. Up until the 1920s, water from the creek had been used to fill the lock in Chesapeake City that either lifted or lowered boats on their journey through the canal. But the C&D was a sea-level canal now, leaving Back Creek to meander its lazy way deep into the marsh. The creek was rumored to have been the lair of bootleggers and even of Blackbeard's pirates, who buried treasure there for safekeeping. They must have done a good job, because nobody had found any gold yet, even after generations of boys—and more than a few grown men—had gone looking for it in the marsh. Mostly, Back Creek was home to blue herons and the occasional kayaker.

I pulled into the driveway, gravel crunching under my tires. Pete's old black lab, Picasso, came rambling around the corner of the cottage, letting loose a couple of deep-throated barks before he recognized me and offered his head for a good scratch. Picasso's tail wagged happily and he snuffled at me with a gray-flecked muzzle.

"Some guard dog, huh?" Pete called from the doorway of his studio.

"That dog is so old he ought to be collecting Social Security," I said, starting toward the studio with Picasso panting at my heels.

Pete's two-bedroom cottage was just the right size for him and Picasso. The oversized shed a few steps from the cottage made it a perfect arrangement for an artist's studio. I stopped to consider Pete's home with professional interest. The small house did not have any particular architectural style, but had been built years ago along modest lines. The house was basically shaped like a shoebox with a roof, and not a whole lot bigger. The cottage had been the retirement home for the owners of the James Adams Floating Theatre, who had spent decades traveling the Chesapeake Bay bringing entertainment to small waterfront towns before finally settling in Chesapeake City. The floating theatre had been the inspiration for Edna Thurber's novel *Showboat* and the consequent Broadway musical. White clapboards clad the exterior walls and the low-pitched roof was covered in cedar shingles. A row of divided light double-hung windows at the back of the house overlooked the creek and marsh, with distant views of the canal. I could just see the funnel of a passing tug.

The shed that housed Pete's studio was styled similarly to the house, with the same clapboard siding and shingles. The roof, however, was higher and steeper. It was crowned by a copper weathervane in the shape of a fish. Pete leaned against the doorway and lit a cigarette.

The first puff set off a phlegmy smoker's cough. "Got to die of something, right?"

I shrugged. With the possible exception of my children, I didn't feel qualified to lecture anyone about their vices. "Sorry about just showing up like this," I said. "I don't mean to keep you from your work."

"Not at all. I could use a break." Pete's faded jeans and

denim shirt were splattered with paint. Spots of color coated his hands and fingers. "Come on in."

The interior smelled strongly of paint and fresh cut wood. Pete built all the frames and stretched the canvas himself. Skylights spilled natural light across the interior. A bank of windows faced northeast, toward the marsh and creek. With a contented groan, Picasso settled onto a scrap of carpet positioned in a patch of sunlight. Paintings in various stages of completion were propped in the corners. Shelves held a collection of props for his historical paintings: swords, military coats with brass buttons, tri-corner hats, brass doorknobs, a cannonball, antique tools and books filled with old photos and illustrations. From the rafters, Pete had hung an entire birch-bark canoe. It must have been a prop once for a painting; now the canoe overflowed as a storage bin, holding deer antlers, walking sticks, a broadsword, a World War I doughboy helmet, rolled maps, a stuffed red fox and various articles of vintage clothing. Pete's studio looked as if a time machine had exploded.

It wasn't my first visit to the studio, but that didn't mean I was used to it. Pete noticed my wide eyes as I took in all the clutter and laughed. "It is a bit much, isn't it? But you never know when something will be useful, and some of these props are so damned hard to get in the first place."

I thought about the shed at the back of the Cosden House, stuffed with old house castoffs nobody knew what to do with yet. "I know just the place to do my Christmas shopping for you."

Pete laughed. "You don't still plan to be in town when December rolls around, do you? That house should be finished by then."

"At the rate we're going, it's hard to say. The owners want it done in time for Canal Day. We'll see."

Pete nodded. "Canal Day. Biggest day of the year in Chesapeake City. Bigger than Christmas, if you make a buck off the tourist trade. I try to paint a new scene or two every year that I can sell then. Here, let me show you."

I followed Pete to a work table covered with several boxes. "I just got these in. See what you think."

Pete began taking out the prints of his Chesapeake City scenes. Some showed ships passing beneath the town's landmark arched bridge. Others were depictions of the town's historic streets with flags flying from every front porch. A couple of other prints were paintings of old-time scenes in town: the Ericcson Line steamer passing through the canal lock, horsedrawn carriages in the streets, a Chesapeake Bay buy boat unloading at the town wharf. Buy boats were small sailing ships that carried Eastern Shore produce to markets in Baltimore and Philadelphia. In the painting, a figure stood upon the bow, hands on hips as if supervising the work. This last print could very well have depicted one of Captain Ezra Cosden's vessels. Pete seemed to read my mind. "I figured that if I don't sell out of this one on Canal Day, then maybe I can get every Cosden in town to buy a copy. I'll tell them that's old Ezra himself on the bow."

I squinted at the figure on the bow. "Is it?"

Pete shrugged. "When it comes to art, sometimes you're better off leaving a little something to the imagination. Let people fill in their own blanks."

"I like it. Frame one for me, will you?"

Pete laughed. "Hell, for you, I'll even sign it." He carefully repacked the boxes. "You know, this isn't my best work, but it helps pay the bills. There's a real market for local nostalgia, and I probably sell more prints like this on Canal Day than I do during the whole year."

"Sounds like a big day." I had yet to experience Canal Day, but I knew that Pete—like a lot of other artists, artisans and jewelry makers—took out tables at the street festival. With the streets closed to traffic in the historic district, the village was transformed into a huge street bazaar. The shops in town would also do a good business, and I knew Pete had paintings and prints on commission in several shops, such as the Magpie.

Canal Day sounded like fun. If we were lucky, and we actually got the Cosden House finished by then, we could enjoy ourselves that day. Otherwise we might all be out looking for jobs.

"Let's just say that on Canal Day I usually make enough to pay my rent right through the summer. Then the holiday season starts. But I've got my work cut out for me getting ready for the big day. I've got to sign and number all these prints, and then try to frame a good number of them. There are always a few people who just want to buy a print, but there's more profit margin in it for me to sell them a framed print."

"I guess I never realized that even an artist has to think like a merchant."

"You kiddin' me? Being an artist of any kind is the toughest business there is." He took one last puff of the cigarette and crushed it out in an antique brass ashtray. "Everybody thinks you're lounging around wearing a beret, but you've got to work the angles if you want to eat. You ought to think about taking out a table."

"Me?"

"Sure. You could sell DVDs of your work on the Cosden House. Hell, put Jenny out there and you could sell just about anything. Where's she been, anyway?"

I shrugged, trying to appear unconcerned. "Oh, Jenny had to take a few days off to take care of some personal business."

"Like I said, if she sets up shop on Canal Day in some skimpy shorts you'll have plenty of customers." Pete grinned. "Me included."

"I'm not so sure about that," I said. "Our show might have worn out its welcome in Chesapeake City."

He nodded. "I heard about the slashed tires. And the brick through the window. Not to mention poor old Iver getting pushed down the stairs."

"You've heard it all then."

"News travels fast in a small town, my friend. I heard Iver told the police that a woman pushed him, which is interesting.

You think this mystery woman slashed the tires and threw the brick?"

I shook my head. "No. As a matter of fact, I'd put my money on Rory Cosden."

Pete raised his eyebrows. "Yeah?"

"He was ready to come after us last night with a hunting knife until Mac ran him off."

"That's some serious shit. Rory, huh? That doesn't surprise me, though. Was he drunk?"

"That would be my guess."

"Some of those Cosdens still brew moonshine, back in the woods and marshes. The rumor is that Rory makes a little himself. That stuff is not to be confused with chardonnay. It'll make you crazier than a blind cat in a rat cage." Pete snorted. "The only reason to make moonshine is because you're ornery. You can still go to jail, not to mention poison yourself if you get the mix or the equipment wrong, and you don't make any money. If you're gonna go to all that trouble, what you should do is grow yourself a nice patch of weed."

"I'll keep that in mind if the renovation business doesn't work out."

Pete laughed again. "Now, I know you're a busy man. You didn't come all the way out here to hear about Canal Day and moonshine."

"As a matter of fact, Pete, I've got a business proposition for you."

He flopped into a ragged upholstered chair. "Shoot."

I had been thinking about it for a while now, so I explained to Pete what I wanted. A painting of the Cosden House in the early 1900s, when horses would have passed in the street and sailing vessels would still have passed by in the canal. It seemed like the perfect gift for the owners—plus it would be a cool addition to our website.

Pete wasn't one to turn down work. We agreed on a price—commissioned work didn't come cheap, but I appealed to his sense of historic restoration and civic duty. Plus I would pay cash.

"I'll work up a few sketches and you can see what you think," he said. Pete stood and cast a glance at his easel, which I took to be a signal that he wanted to get back to work.

We shook on the deal, Picasso thumped his tail vaguely when I scratched the old dog's ears, and then I left him to his paints and brushes while I drove back to my own work in progress. On the way, I mused about the era Pete was going to capture on canvas. I had looked up a few facts about 1913, the year our project house was built. It was the year that Woodrow Wilson became president. The Panama Canal was completed and stainless steel was invented. The New York World published the first crossword puzzle. It was also the year that welcomed Richard M. Nixon and actor Lloyd Bridges, and when the world bid farewell to abolitionist Harriet Tubman, born on a Maryland farm in 1820. Had the workers on our project house sat down at lunch to read the newspaper accounts of the fiftieth anniversary commemoration of the battle of Gettysburg taking place in July? All in all, Pete's painting seemed like a perfect housewarming gift, assuming we finished the project.

CHAPTER 12

The next morning dawned bright and clear, one of those perfect spring days full of promise. Or so I told myself as we rolled out of the motel parking lot. This morning, however, our mini convoy wasn't headed to Chesapeake City. Deputy Sullivan had the day off, so we were going to tape the show at her place today. I felt like a field trip would do us good, even with all the work to do at the Cosden House. We needed some fresh air and new scenery to clear our heads.

The deputy said her house needed some routine maintenance and that's just what we were going to do.

"You're awfully chipper this morning," said Kat, who had been relegated to riding shotgun in my truck because Mac was still in his grumpy mode and had piled into the work van rather than be forced to converse with me. It was plain to see that there was something going on between the two of us, but Kat had the good sense not to bring it up. She was sometimes wise beyond her years, which I had noticed before.

"I can't wait to see this house," I explained. "From what Deputy Sullivan said, it's pretty special. That's the best part about this job, you know, getting invited into someone's home. So many of these old houses have stories to tell."

Kat nodded, though I could see she wasn't quite convinced. She was way more interested in filming than in fixing up a house. I tended to forget that Kat wasn't much older than my

own kids, a fact I was reminded of as she slumped in the front
seat, still sleepy eyed. In the morning light she looked every bit
of her nineteen years—which was to say, awfully young. Kat
didn't drink coffee, but had a Mountain Dew gripped in one
hand. In the other she had a cell phone and was texting
somebody. It reminded me that Iggy and I had talked about
setting up a program to text viewers whenever we had a new
episode or a blog update. Just one more way to promote
Delmarva Renovators. We'd have to work on that. But it was
tough to get everything done when you were producer, carpenter and marketing department all rolled into one.

Following Deputy Sullivan's directions, I turned down a
long lane, gravel crunching under the tires. The van and
Marsha's Saab pulled in behind me. A quarter-mile later,
following the lane through tall stands of tulip poplars, the
gravel road emptied out into a farmyard. A police cruiser was
parked to one side, so I knew we had the right house. Then
Deputy Sullivan came striding out from around a corner of the
house, a large dog at her heels.

"Right on time," she said, tugging on the dog's collar to
keep him from slobbering all over us. He was some kind of
indeterminate breed, brown and white and shaggy. There was
some St. Bernard in there, and maybe even some pony. "This is
Glock, by the way. He doesn't bite, but he is what you might
call drool-challenged."

"Glock?"

"You know, as in nine millimeter."

I didn't know, and I didn't really care, because I had already
lost interest in the dog as soon as I determined that he wasn't
going to snack on any of my body parts. I was more captivated
by Deputy Sullivan's appearance. No uniform today. She wore
worn jeans that hugged her hips and legs, spotted here and
there with a dab of old paint, a sleeveless T-shirt and hair
blowing loose in the morning breeze. No clunky glasses, either,
to hide her big blue eyes. So this was how the deputy looked
out of uniform? Talk about drooling. I was about to give Glock

a run for his money in that regard.

As if on cue, the dog broke loose of the deputy's grip on his collar and bounded toward Mac, who had just gotten out of the van.

"Glock!" the deputy called with a touch of alarm in her voice. The dog had gotten up the kind of speed that might have been attack mode.

Not to worry. As the dog skidded to a stop, Mac reached for Glock's big, square head and rubbed behind the dog's ears. The trickle of drool became a waterfall. Dogs always liked Mac. Maybe they sensed that big and scowling as he was, Mac was just a softie who couldn't wait to scratch behind their ears. He walked toward us, Glock bounding at his side. His shirt this morning read, "Strangers have the best candy."

"I see you made a friend," Deputy Sullivan said. "His name is Glock."

"Please tell me you don't have a cat named Smith and Wesson," Mac replied.

The deputy laughed. I could see that her appearance wasn't lost on Mac, either. "Nope, just me and Glock. I do have a Smith and Wesson, but not the kind you need a litter box for."

"Call me old-fashioned, but I always liked the thirty-eight more than the Glock. At least you can tell when the damn thing is loaded."

The deputy nodded, apparently impressed that Mac knew something about guns. They chatted for a minute about weaponry. Deputy Sullivan—I couldn't quite bring myself to think of her as Maureen—perked up when she learned Mac had been a cop long before he became a contractor.

Behind me, I could hear the rest of the crew shuffling around, getting the lay of the land. There weren't any neighbors to speak of, only fields just turning green with corn and soybeans. A large barn stood not far from the house. In the fields beyond, spring was beginning to take hold. Forsythia and dogwoods bloomed in the hedgerows. The landscaping around the house itself was simple, limited to a few tulips and azaleas.

It was as if the landscaping wasn't even going to try and compete with the massive sycamore tree that stood just beyond the front door. I'd done some research the night before into Deputy Sullivan's place and read that the tree was four hundred years old—a fact that I'd taken with the proverbial grain of salt. But seeing it now, the ancient sycamore looked as if it had weathered every year of four centuries.

Then there was the house. Deputy Sullivan had dropped off some information about the place yesterday. Most of it was copied from various local histories and even an architectural history of Maryland's Eastern Shore. Her house dated back to the eighteenth century. In historical terms, it was the real deal. It even had a name: Elk Knoll. Not that there were any elks in evidence. The name came from the nearby Elk River, which you could just glimpse from the second floor when the leaves were off the trees, and the fact that the house stood on a slight elevation compared to the surrounding fields. On Maryland's Eastern Shore, it was what passed for a hill.

Elk Knoll had started out as two log cabin-style rooms separated by a roofed breezeway. It was a pioneer architectural style known as a dogtrot house. Not so common in the Chesapeake Bay area, but more so down South. This original log cabin had been dated to the 1750s. Around 1815, a second floor was added and the breezeway was filled in to create a third room downstairs. A winding staircase squeezed into the former breezeway now led upstairs. The rough fieldstone chimneys of the log cabin were replaced with brick fireplaces and chimneys. Sometime in the late 1800s, a single-story addition was added to give the house the convenience of an attached kitchen, rather than the free-standing kitchen of a previous era.

The result was a somewhat grand house by nineteenth century standards. Indeed, it had been home to a series of prosperous farmers, including one who served part-time as the local constable during the Revolutionary War. As if to keep the house from putting on airs, however, most of the exterior was covered in rough sawn planking rather than clapboard siding. Gray and weathered, the siding was in desperate need of repair, which was why Deputy Sullivan had called us in. It was a job that was too big for her, and she wanted somebody to help who had some expertise with old houses. You couldn't very well cover a pre-Revolutionary house in vinyl siding. There were people who did, but I don't know how they could sleep at night. In addition to the house, the other major repair issue at Elk Knoll was that the barn had a hole in the roof. All it needed was some plywood and fresh shingles, but sheepishly, Deputy Sullivan had admitted that she didn't do heights.

I looked around at the house, ancient Sycamore, barn and fields. She must have seen my wide eyes surveying what was really a modest plantation.

"Pretty good spread for a local deputy, huh?" she said. "Bet you're wondering if I'm on the take."

"No—"

"The house was sort of in the family," she explained. "My second cousin—my great-great cousin, I suppose, because the old dear was almost ninety—sold it to me with a relative's discount to keep it in the family. But all I've got is three acres with the house and barn. The rest of the land was sold off years ago. The farmer who bought the land put it all in ag preservation, thank God. That means I won't be surrounded by houses."

"Beautiful place," said Mac, still looking a little dazed. Mac loved old houses as much as I did and could get dazzled by them. It was just as likely that he was dazzled by this knockout deputy who liked to talk about guns.

"It's a lot to keep up for just me and Glock," she said. "On a deputy's salary, to boot. My dad helps out a lot. He'll be coming by later this morning. He keeps the grass cut and fixes things, but he'd be the first to tell you that he's more of a handyman than a carpenter."

"Well, Maureen, that's why we're here," Mac said, giving her a big grin.

"Sully," she said. "That's what my friends call me."

"Sully," Mac said, trying it out. "It suits you."

By now, Iggy and Kat had the camera gear out of the truck. Glock had made his introductions, nuzzling everyone one by one. Marsha stared in dismay at the slobber he left on her hand.

Mac and I assessed the siding. Unlike clapboards, where the edges of each horizontal board overlapped to create a barrier against the weather and a sloped surface to shed rain and snow, the siding on Elk Knoll was made of boards set edge to edge. The weakness of this siding method was that wood had a natural tendency to expand and contract, thus opening gaps between the boards that let in moisture. Each board was about eight inches wide and at least an inch thick. Cedar siding, with its natural resistance to rot and insects, lasted indefinitely. But cedar was not a common wood in this region, while oak trees grew in abundance, so it was no surprise that the siding appeared to be cut from oak.

The oak had indeed worn like iron, but was giving in to time and the elements. It didn't help that the bottom course of boards was flush with the soil. Not even oak could last long in contact with the damp earth and most of the lowermost boards were punky with rot. Higher up, carpenter bees had drilled dozens of holes, opening up the wood to further infiltration by the elements. A greenish moss not unlike that found on the north side of trees covered the side of the house oriented in that direction. In short, Elk Knoll was a house in need of serious repair.

"Well, what do you think?" the deputy finally asked, watching us with concern, arms folded on her chest. It wasn't unlike how someone looked as they awaited bad news from their doctor.

"Lots of moisture damage here," I said. To make my point, I prodded one of the lower boards with a screwdriver. It sank into the rotten oak like a knife going into warm butter.

"You've probably got termites too, with this kind of rot.

We'll know more when we pull some boards off."

"Can you do anything?" she asked.

I laughed. "That's why we're here. Mac?"

Mac made a point of ignoring me and addressing his comments to Sully. He wasn't in any hurry to stop being mad at me.

"The hardest part will be finding new boards to replace this wood," Mac said to the deputy. "I'll bet this siding is at least seventy years old, maybe older. Oak like that doesn't exist today, except for fine carpentry. And it costs a small fortune."

"What would you say if I told you I've got a whole stack of these boards in the barn, good as new?"

"Then we're in business," Mac said. "I'll go have a look."

"While you're at it, would you mind checking out the hole in the barn roof?" she asked. "I'm worried that if we get a few more heavy rains, it's really going to do a number on the barn."

Mac headed toward the barn, Glock at his heels. Iggy went with him, lugging a camera and offering to hold the ladder. The two of them did all our high work. I couldn't climb a two-story ladder, much less explore a barn roof, without my legs turning to rubber and my head spinning with vertigo. Heights and spiders were my Achilles' heel when it came to renovation.

Sully ran a hand over the siding. The boards were rough-sawn, without the smooth finish we had come to expect from home center lumber. "A thought occurs to me, Tom. Even if we replace the boards, aren't they just going to rot all over again?"

"Yes and no," I said. "You've got to consider a couple of things. First of all, like Mac said, this siding has been on here for seventy years, maybe longer, which means somebody slapped it up in, oh, about 1930. Even if we just replace the boards that need it, none of us would have to worry about this siding again in our lifetimes. That'll be a job for your grand-kids."

"None of those on the horizon at the moment."

Not knowing what to say to that, I didn't comment. "I've

got another couple of thoughts. One is that we replace the bottom boards with an inert construction material. Water proof, rot proof, insect proof."

"That way it won't pull moisture out of the ground and rot the boards above it."

"Exactly," I said. "The other thing we can do is stain the wood. Use something with a wood preservative, like a deck stain, and the siding will last that much longer. Plus the old boards will then match the new ones. No weathering required."

She nodded. "I think that's a good plan."

I got Kat started setting up so we could film us taking off the first boards. We looked up at the sound of a truck coming. It was a dusty white pickup, and for a moment I worried it was be Rory Cosden.

"That's Dad," said Maureen. "Come on, I'll introduce you."

Marty Sullivan turned out to be in his late fifties or early sixties, burly through the shoulders but a good six inches shorter than his tall daughter. He wore jeans, battered work boots and a T-shirt stretched over his beer gut. A large oval belt buckle decorated with the head of a deer seemed to hold everything in place like an upholstery tack. Mr. Sullivan was be soft in the middle, but he must have done more around Elk Knoll than his daughter let on, because his arms were well muscled and his grip when we shook hands was like a vise. He didn't let go right away but made a point of glancing from Sully to me, with a look that seemed to say *watch it, buddy*. I couldn't help thinking that if every guy since she was sixteen had had to run the daddy gauntlet, it was no wonder that Deputy Sullivan lived at Elk Knoll with nobody but her large guard dog to keep her company.

When he saw Kat setting up her camera and Marsha flouncing around in an outfit better-suited to an office than a work site, sketchbook in hand as she worked up some landscaping ideas, an amused smile flashed across Marty's face. "Huh," he said. "This is going to be interesting. What did you have in mind?"

I summed up our approach to the house, and he nodded in approval. "All right, then. Let's get started."

The camera rolled while Marty and I used pry bars to get the first boards off. The wood mostly crumbled. Some of the more stubborn boards were held in place by square-cut nails that made me wonder if the siding had been put up even longer ago than we first thought.

Before we got too far along, Mac came back from his assessment of the barn. After a quick introduction to Marty Sullivan, he gave us his report. The replacement boards inside the barn did indeed look almost new, and there were plenty of them.

"What about the roof?" Sully asked.

"There we've got a problem," Mac said. "A snake. Big one. Up in the rafters. What I'm wondering is, can I use your gun to take out the snake? I've got a clear shot from the ladder. He's not moving much. Must be sleeping. But there's no way Iggy and I are working on the roof with that thing crawling around up there. That sucker must be six feet long."

The deputy's voice was full of doubt. "I don't know—"

"Hell, girl, let your new friend have some fun," her father said. He turned to Mac. "You know how to shoot?"

"I used to be a cop," Mac said.

This time I echoed the deputy. The thought of clumsy Mac up on a ladder with a gun did not reassure me. "This might not be—"

"See, he knows how to shoot," the father said. "Go get him a gun, honey. If there's one thing I hate, it's a snake. I take a shovel to 'em whenever I see them things around here."

With all the anti-snake opinions swirling around, this didn't seem like the time for me to point out that snakes really were beneficial in that they caught mice and so forth. Snakes I didn't mind. But Mac and Marty and Iggy had gotten themselves up to what amounted to a reptilian lynch mob—not that I'd ever known Iggy to be afraid of snakes when it came to filming the show. Sully went inside and returned soon after with a revolver and a box of shells. Expertly, Mac flipped open the cylinder to make sure it wasn't loaded. With a grin, he headed back to the barn.

"I think this is less about snakes and more about boys having fun," Sully remarked. From the look on her face, she seemed to be having second thoughts about handing her gun over to Mac. "Be careful."

We got back to work on the house. The deputy kept throwing worried glances at the barn. Soon after, we heard shots from that direction. We stopped what we were doing to watch. In the distance, we could see Mac high up on the ladder, shooting through the open vent in the barn gable. Six shots carefully spaced, as if Mac was making each one count. How many bullets did it take to kill a snake?

Once Mac had emptied the gun into the barn, he stared for a moment through the gable vent. "Must have missed!" we heard him shout. Then he seemed to fiddle with the revolver, apparently reloading up on the ladder. He reached into his pocket for the box of shells, but in the process must have lost his grip on the revolver. He seemed to be juggling, and then something fell. Mac lunged after it. One foot slipped off the rung of the ladder in the process.

Watching beside me, Sully gasped.

Too late, Mac realized his mistake and tried to regain his balance. He swayed, the ladder bouncing under his weight. And then Mac half slid, half tumbled to the ground. We couldn't see how he had landed because a row of forsythia obscured our view. I dropped my pry bar and sprinted toward the barn, Deputy Sullivan right behind me.

Please, God, don't let him be dead, I thought. *Or crippled.* Mac and I had been through our share of accidents and injuries. We had a history of broken bones and bleeding. But this looked bad.

I got there just ahead of the deputy. Mac lay on the ground, groaning. I did a quick scan for broken bones or blood, but to my relief didn't see either one. Still, if Mac had hit the ground hard, internal injuries might not be that obvious.

"Don't try to move," Sully said, using her deputy-in-charge voice. "Can you breathe all right?"

"Yeah." Mac put a hand to his head. "Ouch. Must have banged it on the way down."

I turned to Iggy. "What happened?"

"I was holding the ladder," he said defensively. "He dropped the gun and lost his balance."

"We saw that part," I said. "What I mean is, how did he land?"

"He slid most of the way down. That bush right there broke his fall."

I looked to where Iggy had nodded. Indeed, a huge clump of lilac at the foot of the ladder was positively flattened. The lilacs were an ideal cushion. A little to the left, and Mac would have fallen on a hunk of abandoned farm machinery with nasty-looking rusty edges. To the right, a mulberry bush was hacked off mostly to the ground—the jagged stumps would have impaled him. The thought made me shudder.

"You're breathing, you're talking, no bleeding. Okay," the deputy said. "I'm not going to call an ambulance just yet."

"I think I'm all right," Mac said. He made an attempt to sit up and Sully helped him, one hand on his shoulder and one beneath his back.

"Easy," she said.

Mac was sitting with his back against the ladder. It was now apparent to all that landing on the lilac had saved his life, or at least kept him from serious harm. "Whew, that was a close one," he said. "I banged my head on the way down, but that was the worst of it."

"You scared the hell out of us, Mac," I said.

"I knew I shouldn't have let you have that gun," Sully reprimanded herself.

"I hope I got that snake," he replied. "Who says black snakes aren't dangerous? That one almost killed me."

After a few more minutes, it was clear that Mac really had

been spared serious harm.

Marty Sullivan had come running to the barn like everyone else, but had since trotted back to the house. He returned in his pickup truck, taking a shortcut through the field. He got out with a bag of frozen peas in one hand. "I hope nobody was planning on peas for dinner," he said.

Sully took the frozen vegetables from him and eased them onto Mac's forehead, where a good-sized bump was sprouting. "I'm taking you to the ER, just in case," she said. "You need to get that head X-rayed."

"I don't want to sit around the ER—"

"No arguing, big guy," she said in that deputy tone again. "You don't want me to get out the handcuffs. Now get in the truck."

Deputy Sullivan helped ease him into the passenger seat and shut the door. "We'll be back whenever," she said. "I'll call with an update."

CHAPTER 13

We watched the truck bump back over the field to the gravel driveway and then head toward the road. Deputy Sullivan wasn't speeding, not exactly, but she left a cloud of dust in her wake.

"That's one take-charge girl," Marty Sullivan remarked with admiration in his voice. "She never gets shook up."

Iggy found the revolver not far from the ladder. The box of shells had burst open somewhere up above and rained down cartridges, so I spent a few minutes helping him collect the bullets. We didn't want them lying around for a run-in with a lawnmower or maybe being found by a child. As for the bush that had broken Mac's fall, it was a mass of broken branches.

"That was the last of the lilac that in the barnyard bloomed," Iggy remarked.

I groaned. "Walt Whitman must be rolling over in his grave right about now."

What about the snake? For all the trouble this particular reptile had caused, I sure hoped Mac had plugged that sucker full of holes. I wanted to take a look, but I wasn't about to ascend the ladder Mac had just fallen off. Instead, I walked around and entered the barn through the huge double doors that faced the house.

Inside, the barn smelled like moldering hay and saddle leather left to dryrot. There was a distant, half-forgotten odor of horses that might have been left over from another century. Sunlight slanted down through the gable vents, creating bands of light flecked with floating dust. It was clear that Deputy Sullivan didn't use the barn much, except for storage. A large riding mower occupied one corner, along with a collection of hand tools hung neatly along one wall. Rakes, shovels, mattocks, a scythe. Most looked like antiques, their handles worn smooth, polished by generations of farmers' hands.

But it was the old barn's construction that really caught my eye. It was a world apart from the big pole barns with sheet metal roofs and siding, slapped up in a few days, that were now more typical of farm outbuildings.

Technically, this carpentry method could be described as mortise and tenon. Big, square beams hacked out by hand, leaving the wood still rough with marks from an adze blade. Using a hand-held saw, the end of the upright beam was squared off into a tenon that fit into a socket or mortise cut with an auger, mallet and chisel into the horizontal beam, locking the two beams together almost like oversized Lincoln Logs, the joints held together with pegs driven through hand-drilled holes. The labor involved in preparing and then joining two beams using hand tools, not to mention wrestling the heavy log beams into place, was almost unimaginable today in our world of power tools and ready-cut dimensional lumber.

I looked more closely at the construction. What gave a barn its strength and kept it from swaying in the wind or leaning haphazardly after a century of use was the use of cross bracing. Each massive mortise and tenon joint also had a hand-cut brace that ran between the upright and horizontal beams like a shortcut to create a sturdy triangle of wood. The brace was locked into place using more wooden pegs. The resulting timber frame was so sturdy that a barn with a good roof was almost indestructible. I'd even heard of cases where developers clearing old farmsteads to plant a crop of houses ran into the most trouble when it came time to demolish the barn. It took a determined bulldozer or backhoe operator to bring them down. Fortunately, there was now a good market for salvaged barn wood or even the barns themselves, which could be carefully dismantled, the parts labeled, and then reconstructed at a new location.

I faced the ladder that led up to the semi-darkness of the hay loft, a ledge about twelve feet above the barn floor and overhanging perhaps half of the barn's square footage. The ladder looked sturdy, and Deputy Sullivan had assured me that the loft had been in use until a couple of years ago to store bales of straw and hay. I climbed on up, wishing that I'd brought a flashlight, but soon discovered that the sunlight shining down lit the floor of the loft. Stray clumps of hay and scraps of bailing twine littered the floor.

I watched my step. There were supposed to be snakes in here. Looking up, I spotted the snake draped across a rafter several feet overhead. Not exactly an anaconda, but it sure wasn't a garter snake. On closer look, the snake seemed oddly deflated. Maybe Mac had killed it, after all. But as my eyes adjusted to the dim light, I could see that the snake appeared dry and gray, almost papery, though the pattern of scales stood out clearly.

I had to smile. Mac had killed the hell out of a snake skin. I dragged a wooden box out of the corner, where it lay half buried in a drift of hay, and stood on it while I used a pitchfork to snag the snake skin. Sure enough, it was shredded in several places where the bullets had struck it. Mac could still shoot. It was keeping his balance that gave him trouble.

I got down and started to move the box back, noticing that the lid was loose. I used a tine of the pitchfork to open the box—mindful of the fact that snakes got bigger when they shed their skins.

The box appeared to be full of ancient, crumpled newspaper. I prodded inside and struck something that *tinged* against the metal tine. Reaching in, I took out a bottle of whiskey. "Black Cat" said the label. Not a brand I'd ever heard of. Half the bottle was empty. I unscrewed the metal cap and took a whiff. Still smelled all right—I suspected that whiskey never went bad. Some ancestor of Deputy Sullivan's must have kept it up here for medicinal purposes. Maybe during Prohibition? The danger was that if you had too much Black Cat, you still had to negotiate the ladder.

There was something else in the box. I fished around and came out with an oversized Mason jar that weighed about a ton. And no wonder. As I peered into the blue-tinted glass, I realized the jar was packed full of silver dollars. Wow. Now here was a find. Working around old houses, you always heard rumors about how Depression-era people hid their money rather than trusting it to a bank. Not that we'd ever found any of it. Until now.

It took two trips up and down the ladder to haul down the Mason jar, then the whiskey and snake skin. The bottle of Black Cat was a novelty, but the silver dollars must be worth something.

My cell phone rang as I walked back to the house. *Mac.* "What's the prognosis?" I asked.

"Nothing broken. The doc says to take it easy for a few days." He snorted. "Like that's going to happen. We've got a show to do."

"You scared the hell of me, you know."

"I just wanted to get even," he said. "I've been pretty pissed at you since you told me about you and Jenny."

"Yeah? I hadn't noticed."

"Listen, Hammer. I like Jenny a lot. Not in the same way as you, mind you. More like a kid sister." He paused. "You ought to have known better."

"You're right." I was grateful that he'd left the other major factor unsaid, which was that I might have sunk the show.

"We're supposed to be partners in this show, right? So let's make a new rule. No more romantic entanglements. To put it bluntly, no humping the help."

"All right, Mac. Consider it one of our new bylaws."

"Sully and I are going to grab some lunch, and then we'll be back down. You see any sign of that snake?"

"Big sucker. You got him."

"I knew it. See you in an hour or so."

I hung up without saying anything about the snake skin or the silver dollars. I was saving that for when Mac and Deputy Sullivan got back. I had to admit that I was pleasantly surprised that Mac was now speaking to me again. Had a near-death experience given him a change of heart? And then it struck me. *Sully*. I had to smile. I didn't quite buy it when Mac brought up that kid sister stuff about Jenny. I still thought there was an element of the ol' green-eyed monster in there. Jealousy. But evidently he'd found someone—Sully—to take his mind off that.

Nonetheless, it felt good that Mac and I had come to some resolution. We were old friends—friends for longer than my marriage had lasted, in point of fact. The show was secondary to our friendship, but it had been hanging around at the back of my mind that *Delmarva Renovators* wouldn't last long if Mac and I started feuding. True, Jenny was gone, maybe for good. But we were getting by. Without Mac, however, there wouldn't be a show.

At the house, Marty Sullivan was already back at work tugging off the rotted siding. He paused long enough to ask, "Them boys get that snake?"

I held up the snake skin. Marty considered it for a moment, then burst out laughing. "So *that's* what was hanging in the rafters."

"That's not all. Look what else I found." As the others gathered around, I showed off the bottle of whiskey and the coins.

"I'll be damned," Marty said. "What do you think all that silver is worth?"

"We'll have to look it up, but with any luck, this jar of coins will help finance your daughter's repairs."

"Nothing wrong with that." He considered the bottle of Black Cat. "What good is a half-drunk bottle of eighty-year-old whiskey?"

"It'll come in handy if you've got paint brushes to clean."

Marty laughed again and turned his attention back to the siding. One thing about the deputy's father—he didn't like to stand around when there was work to be done. I filed that observation away just in case we needed an extra pair of hands and a strong back as the deadline neared on the Cosden House. I stashed the coins and the whiskey in the truck, then came back out to grab a pry bar and help Marty. The snake skin looked sufficiently alive to hiss and slither once I draped it across a low-hanging limb of the massive sycamore.

We worked hard at it until lunchtime, when Kat came back with subs for everyone from the gas station-deli combo at the intersection with the main road. We were still eating when Mac and Sully returned. Maybe it was just my imagination, but they had this guilty look about them like they'd been up to something. Mac also had a bandage on his forehead where he had whacked it against the ladder. He did a double take when he saw the snake skin.

"Don't tell me—"

"Yep. You hit it, all right. Thing is, that snake wasn't alive in the first place."

"Look at the size of that thing," Sully said, clearly in awe. "It's damn near six feet long. What worries me is that the guy who left his skin behind is still slithering around in my barn somewhere."

"Huh," said Mac. "I vote we call in a roofer to deal with the hole in the barn. Sometimes you have to know when to delegate."

"Agreed," I said. "And I know just where to get the money."

I went to the truck and brought out the coins and the bottle of Black Cat whiskey, explaining that I'd found them in the barn. The jar was so heavy that Sully needed two hands to lift it. "This calls for a celebration," she said. "It's Saturday night, people. We're going out dancing!"

• • •

Channel Cats is one of those waterfront joints with fake palm trees and lots of white mini-lights strung everywhere, to create a sort of tropical Christmas theme. Neon waves splashed across the wall behind the tiki bar, which has a thatched roof and bartenders wearing Hawaiian shirts. A beery, low-tide smell permeated the air. The huge deck overlooked the canal and town harbor, which the locals obstinately called "the mooring basin." Jimmy Buffet would have loved the place. Named for the predatory catfish that cruised the nearby canal, it was the biggest nightclub in Chesapeake City. In summer, the crowd spilled out onto the waterfront terrace. But this time of year, with the last of winter's chill in the night air, a much smaller dance floor was enclosed by a plastic barrier and warmed with portable propane heaters. The dance music was too loud, but a bottle of Yuengling was just two bucks, so Channel Cats got points for that.

"One good thing," Mac mumbled as he looked around. "I doubt there's any line dancing."

With the bandage on his head, Mac looked like an extra from a low-budget disaster movie. He had hurt his head, not his leg, but Mac was limping a bit, which I suspected was for a couple of reasons. First, he was probably hoping it got him off the hook as far as dancing went. Second, it won him constant attention from Deputy Sullivan.

"You just sit here," she said. "The doc said no alcohol or caffeine for a while, so let me get you a lemonade."

Mac nodded, wincing a bit as he did so. I rolled my eyes as Sully scurried off to the tiki bar. We had come right from the jobsite at her farm, but she had taken some time to change. She wore new jeans that fit like a body glove, a tight white T-shirt and red lipstick. Let's just say she left a wake as she cut through the crowd.

Until launching the show, my musical evolvement had ended somewhere around U2's *The Joshua Tree*. I was too busy with work and family to pay much attention to the latest music. But our crew was a bunch of music lovers and some of it had rubbed off on me, so much so that my boys had bought me an iPod for my last birthday. Iggy liked what you might call post-punk. Marsha went for classical music and modern folk. Kat was into everything, which was why I recognized some of the songs blaring over the Channel Cats speakers. Fergie.

Kat popped out of her chair and grabbed Iggy's hand. "Let's go," she said.

The two of them eased onto the dance floor. Iggy had a couple of moves, but mostly he sort of jerked his body and bobbed his head up and down. It was like watching a giant raven peck something to death. Kat had the whole dancing thing down, bare arms upraised as she did a slithery bop to a Justin Timberlake song.

"Damn, she looks good out there," Mac shouted over the music. "Who knew our little Kat could groove."

I was pretty sure using "Kat" and "groove" in the same sentence was some sort of *faux pas*, but I let it go.

"Come on, you two," Marsha said. "Don't tell me you're going to sit there like a couple of sash weights."

"Excuse me?" Mac said. "That's insulting. I'm more like an antique door stop."

I obliged Marsha by getting out on the dance floor. The crowd was mostly younger, so I wowed them with the arm and leg thing from the grapevine and a few steps from "The Hustle." Marsha laughed and bumped my hip.

The music changed to Lady Gaga's *Poker Face*. Kat switched over and danced across from me while Marsha and Iggy paired up. Iggy and Kat had danced a polite distance apart, like a couple of co-workers or maybe an uncle and niece at a wedding. Not Iggy and Marsha. To my surprise, they got up close and personal. Not dirty dancing, or not exactly, but it made me wonder if I'd been missing something going on between those two. Maybe my fling with Jenny hadn't been the only behind-the-scenes romance.

Mustang Sally. Sully appeared on the dance floor towing Mac by one hand. He was really hamming up the limping thing, but the off-duty deputy was having none of that. Sully looked good out there. I was beginning to realize she would look good just about anywhere. Opposite her, Mac kind of lurched around, bumping into other dancers. One or two guys looked annoyed enough to make an issue of it, but Mac was a good head taller and resembled an SUV in a parking lot full of economy cars. And with the bandage on his head, he could have passed for a crazy man. They did their dancing elsewhere, until Mac had a kind of empty safety zone around him on the dance floor.

A slower song came on, something I didn't recognize, and the dance floor quickly emptied. I made a beeline for the bar to get another round of Yuenglings for everybody. I'd once heard that there were few problems in life that couldn't be solved by buying another round, and at the moment, I'd have to agree.

By the time we finished those beers, and downed a platter of nachos, it was getting late. Sully lured me away to dance a few songs, but the whole time I was out there I felt like I was getting the stink eye from Mac. The last thing I wanted to do was jeopardize our fragile truce, so the first chance I got I slipped back to our table. Another round—at least for those who weren't driving—and we got up to go. We had work to do the next day on our behind-schedule project house. I didn't know about everyone else, but I was actually eager to get started in the morning. We had the kitchen floor to finish, not to mention the cabinets . . . and the trim work . . . and the . . . well, we had plenty to keep us busy.

In the parking lot, we said goodbye to Sully, piled into the work van and Marsha's car, and then headed back to the hotel. I grabbed a quick shower and gratefully tumbled into bed. I was getting too old for this work all day, dance all night routine, because I fell asleep before my head hit the pillow.

Rory got dressed while the coffee pot burbled on the counter.

"Another day, another dollar," he said to no one in particular. He was doing that more and more, he realized. Talking to himself. There he went again. It came from living alone. But these days he didn't feel like doing much of anything, let alone seeing anyone. Rory wondered if maybe it was time to get another dog. His last one had run off, the ungrateful mutt. He debated calling up Tom Martell. He wanted to warn him, tell him to stop digging up the past. It was the kind of thing a man had to do face to face. Rory knew he had tried that before, but he had lost his temper. This time around, he was determined to stay calm. Maybe even sober.

He bent down to pull on his boots and the rush of blood to his head didn't do his hangover any favors. Got to get off the sauce, he thought. Every morning he made a pledge to himself that he was going to drink less. But by evening, when the blues and the loneliness came on . . . well, there was nothing like a few glasses of good ol' Canal Town moonshine to mellow him out.

Rory finished lacing up his boots just as his coffee pot was winding down. He stomped over and poured himself a mug. Sipped. "Strong," he said out loud before he could catch himself. There he went again. Shaking his head, coffee mug in hand, he wandered into the spare bedroom. He still thought of it as the spare bedroom, even though he wasn't expecting any guests, and Rory had long since converted it into something else.

Some days, when he wasn't working, he went in there to paint. This morning, he was content just to sip his coffee, feeling the caffeine kick in and go to work on his hangover.

He looked around at the photographs and paintings. Some of the places and scenes were long gone, the people too, but to Rory it all still seemed very much alive. They were like old friends. He took a big drink of coffee and felt a sense of satisfaction about the collection he had worked years to build.

Rory was thinking about refilling his coffee mug when somebody knocked at the door of the trailer. "Now who could that be?" he wondered out loud. The neighbors tended to steer clear of him. He didn't move. Maybe they would think he was asleep and leave him alone.

The knocking became more insistent, so loud that it set his head to aching all over again.

Curious, and more than a little annoyed, he set down his mug and went to answer the door.

It seemed like I had only been asleep a few minutes when the bedside telephone woke me. Six a.m. When the phone rings very early or very late, it had to be something bad. The first thing I thought about was the boys. My voice tight with anxiety, I managed to grunt something like "hello" into the phone. It turned out to be bad news, all right, but not what I expected.

"This is Sully. I thought I'd better let you know that we found Rory Cosden's truck in Back Creek this morning. Looks like he ran off the road." She took a deep breath, then let it out. "He's dead, Tom."

"Good Lord." My first thought was that Rory had been binging on that legendary Cosden moonshine. "Was he drinking?"

"I think you'd better get out here," Deputy Sullivan said.

CHAPTER 14

It looked like the biggest accident Chesapeake City had seen in a long time. Fire trucks and police cars lined the road, their flashing lights giving the morning mist and drizzle an eerie glow. Yesterday's spring weather and sunshine were gone. It was a chilly morning and the dead-fish smell of low tide hung in the air. It didn't help that I'd had one beer too many the night before and not enough sleep. My head seemed to throb in time to the flashing lights.

I had seen my share of accidents early on in my writing career, as a reporter for The Milford Bee & Observer, a small weekly. That had only lasted a year before I got into magazine work, which better suited me. But all these years later, here was the familiar sight of emergency vehicles lined up, bored cops standing around with cups of coffee in their hands, and the stretcher waiting by an ambulance.

"Looks bad," Mac said.

"If you were Rory Cosden, you might be thinking that's the understatement of the year," I said.

Mac was driving, and he wheeled the truck into place behind a police car. He wasn't wearing one of his goofy T-shirts, but had on one of our *Delmarva Renovators* golf shirts instead. We got out, hands shoved in our pockets, and headed closer. The road was closed, and a local member of the fire department was out there with a flashlight that ended in one of those orange plastic wands, turning traffic away. He was an older guy, at least seventy. Too old to ride the fire truck, but with a grizzled face that brooked no argument from inconvenienced motorists. His nylon windbreaker and ball cap read "Fire Police" but he didn't make any effort to stop us, just nodded hello. I guess we looked like we knew what we were doing.

We spotted Deputy Sullivan right away. She was out of uniform, wearing boots and jeans with her hair pulled back, but had on a blue sweatshirt with CCSO—Cecil County Sheriff's Office—in big yellow letters across the back. She waved us over.

"Looks like the accident happened just after daylight," she said. "A jogger called it in."

"Where's the truck?" I asked.

She pointed. Out in the middle of the creek, I could just make out the roof of Rory's pickup. Muddy tidal water covered the truck bed and the windows of the cab. Divers in wetsuits were doing something to the truck. One had a cable in his hand with a hefty hook. It looked like he was trying to figure out the best place to attach it to the truck.

"Tide's coming in," Sully said. "We might have to wait until the water goes down again so we can get the truck out of there."

Mac nodded. "Less resistance."

Even this far up the Chesapeake Bay, the water rose and fell as much as three or four feet between high and low tide. A waterway as shallow as Back Creek was basically reduced to a mud flat at low tide. But it looked like the fire department wasn't going to let a little high water stop them.

"We got the body out," she added. "But we need the truck in case there's any evidence inside."

"What evidence would there be?" I looked around. The road here followed the perimeter of the town harbor. We were standing on the bridge that carried the road across Back Creek. Then the road continued along the water's edge. From the air, the harbor and creek would resemble a ping-pong paddle, with the creek forming the handle. "Looks like a clear case of drunken driving."

Sully and Mac didn't say anything, but only exchanged a look. "What?" I asked.

"Pretty good driving for a drunk," Mac said.

I began to see what he meant. This section of road was basically a straightaway. The approach to the bridge was well-protected by a guard rail. From the tire ruts in the soft ground, it appeared that Rory's truck had left the road before the guard rail, navigated past a clump of trees and splashed into the creek without so much as bending a blade of grass. Rory would have needed all the bad luck in the world to run off the road at that point and not hit anything to slow down the truck before it went into Back Creek . . . or his trip into the creek had been deliberate. "Suicide," I muttered.

"The truck will tell us more," Sully said. "I just thought you should know what happened. I know Rory helped you on the Cosden House for a while, but you've had a couple of run-ins with him since then. I would say he was a troubled individual."

Deputy Sullivan was now the one in the running for Understatement of the Year. She wandered off toward a knot of other cops. Mac and I stood around waiting for the salvage operation.

Rory was troubled, all right, but he had that Cosden instinct for survival. I just couldn't see him deciding to end it all—never mind how much moonshine had addled his brain.

It was hard to know how I felt about Rory. His violent behavior did not endear him to me. I wasn't so vindictive that I wanted to see him dead. But in a way, I wasn't surprised to see his life end in that muddy creek, suicide or not. As Sully had pointed out, Rory had his demons.

He had threatened me directly that night at the Cosden House with his wicked-looking skinning knife. The incident with the knife had surely been fueled by moonshine, or the equivalent. Sober, Rory had likely been the one who had used that same knife to slash our tires. Why? Rory had gotten angry about the changes at the Cosden House, or else he'd become jealous of the newcomers who had the money to take that historical home out of family ownership. Hostility must have made sense to Rory, even if the rest of us didn't see it that way. He was one of those people whose first reaction to anything he didn't like was to get mad about it.

Nagging at the back of my mind, however, was the brick thrown through the window with Leo Cosden's name scratched into it. Had Rory thrown the brick? If so, what message was he trying to send that he couldn't just tell me? I glanced at the submerged truck. Rory wouldn't be around to answer any of these questions.

Out in the creek, we watched the diver with the cable hook disappear beneath the muddy current. He didn't go under completely, because we could still see the back of his wetsuit, as if a seal or a sea monster had made its way into Back Creek. He popped back up, waded a few steps away, and signaled the tow truck driver on shore. A motor began to whir and whine as it retrieved the cable, which pulled taut, dripping water into the creek. I could almost hear it quiver. The truck didn't budge. Then, ever so slowly, the pickup began to creep toward shore. The combined weight of the truck and the water it now held on the cable must have been tremendous. But the drum on the back of the tow truck spun on like a giant fishing reel, slowly and patiently winding in the truck. Soon Rory's old pickup was halfway up the bank, water gushing from the windows and from between the gaps around the doors. Mud clutched at the tires, but the tow truck pulled even those free. Battered and waterlogged, the truck resembled a drowned corpse.

"Rory Cosden," I murmured. "Who would have thought? That guy seemed indestructible as a junkyard dog."

"Something about it just doesn't add up," Mac agreed.

My phone rang. It was Iggy, calling from our project house. I filled him in on Rory, and he seemed duly shocked. "But if you don't get over here soon, the police are going to have another body on their hands," he said, sounding exasperated, which was unusual for him. He dropped his voice and whispered. "The homeowners are here again. And the missus has changed her mind. She wants her clawfoot tub back."

I snapped shut the phone and groaned.

Mac gave me a look. "What?"

"We've got a house to finish," I said. "Beyond that, you really don't want to know."

Sully was busy with the other police so we gave her a wave and took off. No sense hanging around the accident scene. With the truck out of the water and Rory's body gone to the medical examiner in Baltimore, the drama was over. We had seen enough. Mac drove the short distance into town—slowly. From my police reporter days, I knew that there was nothing like visiting the scene of a fatal accident to make you into a careful driver. That also had been the reason we ran those gory accident photos in my newspaper days—as a kind of public service to remind us about being safe behind the wheel. Apparently the bad drivers didn't read the paper because I never ran out of accidents to shoot.

We had an uneventful trip into town. Cindy Pritchard's bright yellow Hummer was parked in front of the Cosden House. I reflected that it must have taken a lot of doggy doo to buy one of those.

"Back me up on this, Mac," I said as we prepared to go inside. "The clawfoot tub is far, far away."

"Yep. On its way to Istanbul for scrap metal."

Cindy bought the story, but not without a round of pouting. "I wish you hadn't gotten rid of it," she said. "It was *my* bath tub, after all. It came with the house, so that makes it historical."

I might have pointed out to Cindy that the ancient wiring and crumbling plaster were just as *historical*, but I bit my tongue. A good renovator knows what to keep, and what to update. Antique plumbing was not high on my list of keepers.

"The local building code says you can't leave plumbing fixtures outside. Not even overnight. We had to haul it away,"

Mac said, lying through his teeth.

I raised my eyebrows at him, but I could tell Cindy's mind had moved on to something else. She wanted to talk shower stalls. I listened for a few minutes, nodding attentively, and then waved Marsha over. She soon had Cindy looking over tile samples, plotting another change in plans for the upstairs bath, the two of them thick as thieves. I managed to slip away.

We had such a long list of work to do that I could take my pick of projects. Yesterday's visit to Deputy Sullivan's house had been an interesting side trip, but it had put us behind, as had Rory's death. The morning fog hadn't lifted, but seemed to hang over the town, weighing down our spirits with a damp gauze. Whatever we did, it seemed wise to choose a project as far away as possible from Cindy. So when she and Marsha went upstairs to reassess the bathroom design, Mac and I headed for the kitchen to start hanging cabinets.

The cabinets were more like fine furniture than something one used to store dishes and spare jars of spaghetti sauce. And believe me, the custom cabinets had cost as much as a new car. The cherry cabinets were finished so that the wood seemed to glow with a light all its own, and the doors featured panes of antique-style glass complete with waves and bubbles to mimic an old window. Such touches of antiquity did not come cheap. Some people thought a window into your kitchen cabinets was more efficient because it enabled you to tell what was inside at a glance. I was more of the school that believed solid cabinet doors were useful for hiding clutter. Back home, our dishes were a mismatched collection of two or three sets, not to mention the oddball coffee mugs and drinking glasses. Boys are hard on dishes. Wistfully, I thought of our own kitchen cabinets—particle board faced in wood-grain plastic laminate. Hardly a renovator's pride and joy, and even downright embarrassing. I'd always meant to replace them with something better, but never quite found the time or money.

We had already marked where the studs were behind the wall and snapped a level chalk line where we wanted the bottom edge of the cabinet to go. Cabinets are heavy—though the doors were off to make them lighter and easier to handle—and it's common practice to attach a board to the wall to create a temporary rail on which the cabinet sits while you screw it into the studs. This rail holds the weight and prevents a lot of the inevitable slipping while one person tries to hold the cabinets in place as the other hangs them. We had used this setup on the opposite wall and Iggy had filmed us doing it the right way. It reminded us again how much we missed Jenny, because she was so good at explaining everything for the camera.

Now the camera wasn't around. We were behind schedule, so we opted to skip the rail and have Mac hoist the cabinets while I wielded the screw gun. *Zip, zip.* The cabinets were up by the time Marsha and Cindy returned downstairs.

"Ooh!" Cindy exclaimed. "They're beautiful! You guys do such great work."

"Just wait till we get the doors on," I told her. "You made such a good choice with these."

"Thanks, Tom. Now, I've been thinking about the tub in the bathroom—"

As if by Divine Providence, someone started knocking on the front door.

"Gosh, who could that be? We better see who it is. C'mon, Mac."

It hardly took two people to answer the door, but Mac and I practically ran out of the kitchen. The last thing we wanted to do was hear Cindy explain to us about how she had changed her mind—again—about the upstairs tub. Cindy didn't know it, but all three hundred pounds of cast iron tub were in the shed out back with our other renovation castoffs. Before she started poking around out there and found the tub, we were going to make it disappear, under cover of darkness if necessary.

Much to our surprise, we found Deputy Sullivan on the front porch. She was now in uniform, hair pulled back, sunglasses on, cruiser parked out front. Hard expression on her face. It looked as if somebody had locked up our renovating and dancing friend Sully, then thrown away the key.

"I've got some news you might want to hear," the deputy-formerly-known-as-Sully said. "The medical examiner says somebody shot Rory Cosden."

"*What?*"

"Now, how 'bout if the three of us take a little ride."

It was clear that this was an order, not a suggestion. I glanced at Mac, who only shrugged, then dumped my screw gun by the front door. We followed Deputy Sullivan down to the Sheriff's Office cruiser and climbed in. Mac got to ride up front.

"I hope you're not arresting us," I said.

Deputy Sullivan glanced at me in the rearview mirror and kind of chuckled. "Why on earth would I do that? You didn't shoot Rory, did you?"

"As a matter of fact, I did not."

"That's what I thought. But you knew him. A little. We're going to investigate his residence to see what we can see."

I noticed that she used cop lingo. *Residence.* "Why us? There are lots of people who knew Rory better. You really need to do your sleuthing without us. In case you haven't noticed, we've got an old house to restore."

"Hey, you're the ones who started this whole mess by finding that body in the wall," the deputy reminded us. "As for Rory, you knew him, but you didn't *know* him. There's a difference. I need someone who isn't local, and who isn't related. That rules out most of the police force."

"Any idea what we're looking for?" I asked.

"It's a little like recognizing a fool," the deputy said, looking at me pointedly in the rearview mirror. "You know one when you see one."

CHAPTER 15

Rory Cosden's address was on Wild Goose Court, which turned out to be a mobile home park a couple of miles outside town. For someone who loved old houses, as I do, the sight of so many grim aluminum boxes set my teeth on edge.

"What in the world are we going to find here?" I wondered.

"Bear with me," Sully said, guiding the county police cruiser down the rutted gravel road. The suspension got a workout as we rolled into one water-filled pothole after another.

It was too early for flowers, but several houses displayed decorative flags or hand-made wooden whirligigs and little Dutch girl cutouts, perpetually bending over to flash their bloomers.

The cruiser's tires crunched to a stop in front of the last trailer on the dead-end street. The bare branches of the wintertime woods, thick with vines, seemed to reach out to claim these last few trailers. Rory's place had none of the niceties of his neighbors'. The muddy patch of yard out front was marked with tire ruts. A rusty washing machine sat on concrete blocks to one side of the trailer. I looked closer and noticed a bright orange extension cord snaking back toward the house. Like a book end, an empty dog house stood at the other side of the trailer. If Rory had kept a pet, it looked to me like his dog had done run off a long time ago.

"Okay," Sully said, getting out. "Let's do this, people."

"The question is, are we supposed to be doing this?" I wondered. "Don't we need a search warrant or something?"

"Technically speaking, what we're doing isn't entirely legal," the deputy said. "But if there are any clues to Rory's death, we're not going to find them on the front step. At the same time, we're not breaking any laws, if that's what you're worried about. Rory Cosden is dead. That means he doesn't have any rights. And since he lived alone, who is going to complain?"

I wasn't particularly comfortable with this line of reasoning, but Sully wasn't interested in a response. She led the way up the rickety wooden steps and gave the door a perfunctory knock, not that we were expecting an answer. The door was not locked, but easily swung open to reveal the dark interior of the trailer. Old houses often have peculiar, musty smells thanks to damp cellars and old wood, but it's a smell that's not altogether unpleasant. Rory's trailer smelled like none of those things. It stank of something gone bad—rotten hamburger and onions came to mind, with some sweat socks or stale beer thrown in. We left the door open behind us to let in a little fresh air.

We fanned out to search the trailer. I had to admit it was more than a little strange, going through the belongings of a dead man—and recently dead, at that. I didn't know what we expected to find, but I agreed with Sully that we'd know it when we saw it.

Rory's home was dark and could have used a good airing out, but it was otherwise fairly neat inside. No piles of junk or dirty laundry. Washed dishes neatly stacked in the drain tray. Everything seemed to have its place and the worn carpet was recently vacuumed. The room was decorated in a style that might be described as "Redneck Bachelor." The one new item was a large flat screen television, hooked to a satellite receiver box. The rest of the furniture seemed to have been gleaned from yard sales and maybe family castoffs. There was a sagging plaid couch with lamps on either side that had been made out of deer hooves, with matching lampshades in hunter's camouflage. A deer's head peered down from the wall with glassy eyes.

Sully saw me admiring the trophy buck. "How could you sit there with that thing making Bambi eyes at you all the time?" she wondered out loud.

Mac was busy taking stock of the fridge. "Beer, peanut butter and jelly, a package of ground beef, a loaf of white bread," he said. "I guess Rory wasn't a gourmet chef. That explains why he was a regular at the café in town."

The kitchen cabinets didn't contain much more than a can of coffee, bag of rice, and several one-can meals in the culinary vein of spaghetti and meatballs, beef stew, and soup.

We moved on into Rory's bedroom. Here again, the furnishings looked battered and worn, but the room was neat enough. A couple of football trophies stood on the particle board dresser, reminders of Rory's high school glory days. The double bed was made, but a sleeping bag was spread on top. From its rumpled appearance, it seemed that Rory must have crawled out of it just that morning. The bedside table contained an old wind-up alarm clock, a water bottle, and a small stack of Playboy magazines. There was an aging Compaq computer with a VDT monitor hooked into the bedroom phone jack. Dial-up? Hadn't seen that in a while. I sat down and fiddled with it until his e-mail came up, but there wasn't much. I checked his history. In the last few days, Rory had visited an online auto parts store, a Chesapeake Bay history site, and a couple of sites that might have been porn.

The second bedroom was where we hit the jackpot. It was as different from the rest of the trailer as sweet was from sour. What Rory had done was transform the spare bedroom into a miniature museum dedicated to local history—and to the Cosden family in particular. One wall was now covered with shelves, on which sat various local artifacts. I recognize bottles from the A.E. Sprague soda bottling plant that had operated for several years back in the early 1900s. Milk bottles from the dairy on the north side of the canal. Photographs in black frames covered two walls. There were shots of the old ferry system that residents had been forced to use when the highway bridge was knocked down by that ship in 1942. Photos of old businesses and public gatherings. Even a class photo of the last graduates of Chesapeake City High School before the school moved to a larger regional school outside town limits. Posters from political campaigns and circus visits. And newspaper clippings—I counted at least twenty, all matted and framed.

The fourth wall was dominated by a large, framed image of Captain Ezra Cosden. Not a photograph, but an oil painting on canvas. Looking closer, I noticed several other paintings around the room, all of Chesapeake City scenes. They were all amateurish compared to the work of someone like Pete Morrison. More like something out of a high school art class.

Sully peered closely at the signature on the nearest canvas. "Rory painted them," she announced. "Who would have thought?"

Surrounding the Captain Cosden's portrait were artifacts strictly related to the Cosden family. A framed needlepoint sampler apparently sewn by Rory's grandmother as a little girl. Wedding photographs. Another painting of a sail-rigged Chesapeake Bay buy boat—apparently Captain Cosden's. Framed deeds in eighteenth-century handwriting. What Rory had done wasn't so much create a museum as make a shrine to the Cosden family. Curiously, I also noticed several intricate mod-els of Chesapeake Bay vessels, everything from skipjacks to a replica of the famous James Adams Floating Theatre. I seemed to recall something about several models going missing from the Chesapeake City Historical Society a while back. Had Rory been the culprit?

"This is incredible," Mac said, trying not to bump into anything. In the cramped confines of the makeshift museum, Mac looked like a giant. The house shook with every step he took, threatening to topple the carefully arranged bottles and ship models.

"I never would have guessed that Rory had it in him," Sully

replied. "He's got quite the museum here. But unless I'm mistaken, every last one of those model ships was reported stolen. I guess that solves one crime."

"I'm glad that Iver Jones is going to get back his models for the historical society, but it would be better if we could figure out why someone murdered Rory," I said.

We kept looking, going through the objects in the museum one at a time. One painting in particular caught my eye. It showed Captain Cosden's ship under full sail, on the azure waters of the Chesapeake, against a sky dotted with cotton ball clouds. I couldn't help but think that it was sad how the family fortunes had faded to the point where one of the captain's descendants had to live in this dismal trailer. To make things worse, poor Rory hadn't seemed able to let go of the past. It all added up to make him bitter toward us and our old house project.

Rory's home hadn't told us much, certainly not why someone would want him dead. But if Rory had created his own museum, he knew more than a little about Chesapeake City history. The question was, had he known something that was worth killing him over?

"I give up," Mac said, easing back into the hallway. "There's nothing useful here unless you like dust and memories."

I couldn't argue with that. Even Deputy Sullivan gave in with a shrug and started out of the room. "We'll head back into town," she said. "There could be new developments."

"What will happen to all this stuff?" I wondered, taking a final glance around Rory's private museum.

"I don't know," Sully said. "I'm sure it's up to the immediate family to dispose of as they see fit."

"Maybe someone should suggest that they box it up and give in to the town's historical society," I said. "It would be a shame to see this stuff go into an attic somewhere, never to be seen again."

"That's a good idea," Sully agreed. "I'll slip the word to a couple of the family members and put a bug in Iver's ear, let him work on them."

We started back through the trailer. Knowing that Rory was dead, the place felt hollow as an empty beer can. It would have been creepy, if I hadn't been used to working around old houses all the time. They were often full of stuff, scraps of the previous lives they had sheltered. Rory's trailer wasn't much different when you thought about it.

"What's this?" Sully had paused by the front door. A bowl on the table there held change and what looked like a spare set of truck keys. There was a stack of mail, too, mostly bills. Unopened. Sully reached down and picked up an envelope. She turned it toward me so that I could see my name marked on it in big block letters. I don't know how we had missed it when we came in.

I took the envelope from Sully. There was a much older sheet of paper inside, folded with creases sharp as a razor, as if the document had spent years pressed between the pages of a heavy book. Mac and Sully crowded in over my shoulder to read it. I couldn't help but be very aware of Sully as she pressed against my arm. She smelled faintly of leather and gun oil with a hint of perfume—Chanel might have a hard time marketing that particular scent, but it was not an unattractive combination for the deputy. I tried to concentrate on what I was reading. I quickly made sense of it. "I'll be damned."

"What?"

"This is a delivery receipt for a Sears Roebuck house."

"A catalog house?"

"Yes," I said, scanning the document. Sears Roebuck and Company had sold thousands of these kit houses around the turn of the last century. They ranged from the modest to the grand. I was no expert on Sears houses, but judging by the price tag on the receipt, this must have been a real showplace. "Delivery was taken in Baltimore. It's signed by Leo Cosden. It's dated October 20, 1913. Does that date ring a bell for anyone?"

Mac knew. "The day of the storm. The nor'easter that sank

Leo Cosden's boat."

"If Captain Leo picked it up that day, then this house must have gone down with the ship," I said. We all stood around a moment, thinking about that. If Leo Cosden's ship had sunk without a trace, there shouldn't have been a delivery receipt for his last cargo. There shouldn't have been a body in the wall, either. If we'd had our doubts before, it was now becoming clear that, in fact, it had been Leo's remains we found in Ezra Cosden's house.

"What in the world is this doing in Rory's house?" Sully wondered.

"Unfortunately, we can't ask him now," I said. "But I can think of somebody who might know."

CHAPTER 16

Sully dropped us at the Cosden House but I grabbed Mac's arm as he headed for the porch steps. "C'mon. Let's return to the scene of the crime."

"Don't we have an old house to work on?"

"In for a penny, in for a pound," I said. "Besides, our homeowner from hell is still here. You want another lecture on the joys of antique bathtubs and how she wants us to put hers back?"

"I'll drive," he said.

News of Rory's death must have spread quickly. On the sidewalks and porches, I could see small knots of neighbors chewing over the news. Rory might not have been well-liked, but he *had* been well known—he was a Cosden, after all—and the manner of his passing was certainly worth talking about. I wondered if it was already common knowledge that Rory had been shot. If not, it would be by the time the local newspaper hit the streets the next morning. That would give Chesapeake City something to talk about all over again.

It was just a short drive out to the curve where Rory's pickup had plunged into Back Creek. I half expected to find a crowd of gawkers, but there was nothing left to see. In the time that Mac and I had spent hanging the kitchen cabinets, the police had finished dragging the pickup out of the creek. Nobody was around, although some cars did pass slowly from time to time, checking out the scene. We parked our truck and got out.

"So if Rory got shot, how did it happen?" I asked Mac. As a former cop, I figured he would have some insight into shootings and guns in general. "Would the shooter have been up close or far away, like a sniper?"

Mac shook his head. "Sully said the bullet was a musket ball."

I shrugged. "I'm no expert on weapons. What does that mean?"

"It means he wasn't sniped from half a mile away," Mac said. "A musket is a short-range weapon. It fires a smooth round bullet. There's no spin on the projectile, like there is with a rifle. You would have to be up close to hit anything with a musket ball."

That was interesting. I nodded, looking out at the muddy water of the creek and thinking about it. A musket seemed more like a weapon one of Blackbeard's pirates would have used—if the legends were true—on a trip up the creek to hide treasure. But Rory hadn't been murdered by pirates. "Maybe the killer shot him, put him in the truck, and drove the truck into the creek."

We looked at each other, then shook our heads. "Nah," Mac said. "Rory was built like a brick and I'd say he weighed a couple hundred pounds. To shoot him and then get him into the truck, you'd have to be strong as an ox and there's too much chance somebody might see you."

"Who in the world still uses a gun that shoots musket balls?"

"Maybe deer hunters," Mac said. "Black powder weapons are popular with them. Or some kind of Civil War reenactor. It could be that it was a stray bullet."

"That doesn't make any sense. It's not deer season and I haven't seen any reenactments going on."

"I'm just saying it's unusual," Mac said. "Let's get back in the truck and make a drive by."

Mac drove over the bridge, turned around, and made another pass from farther out, following the harbor road from town. Houses and wooded yards on the right, the harbor on the left, the water so close you could spit into it. The killer would have been hard pressed to conceal himself. Unless, of course, he had been in plain sight.

Mac slowed down as we approached the bridge. The road followed a curve, so if you were speeding or lost control—let's say because you were shot—it would only be natural for a vehicle to obey the laws of centrifugal force and fly off the road. But the gap between the end of the guardrail and the edge of the bridge was just narrow enough for our truck to pass through. Then Rory would've had to navigate the trees and brush to reach the creek.

"You'd have to drive a stunt car for a living or maybe be a NASCAR racer to hit that just right," Mac commented.

"Let's try it again," I said. "Faster this time."

"It's your funeral."

We crossed the bridge and turned around again. This time as we went around the Harbor Road, Mac gunned it. To my surprise, he took his hands off the steering wheel as we raced around the curve toward the bridge. I grabbed for anything I could hold onto. Our pickup careened around the curb and started to go off the road.

"Mac!"

At the last instant, he stomped on the brakes. Tools and scraps of wood bounced wildly in the truck bed. The truck skidded to a stop just inches from the concrete bridge abutment. I thought something in the engine must have broken free because I kept hearing a *thud, thud, thud* sound. Then I realized it was my heart.

"You said *faster* this time, not suicide speed."

"No blood, no foul," Mac said. "And we just proved something."

"What's that?"

"There's no way Rory ran off the road by accident. If he

lost control, he would've hit the bridge. I'd say someone else drove him into the creek. Here's what I think happened. It was somebody he knew. They got up close, shot Rory, pushed him out from behind the wheel, and drove into the creek. I'd say it happened nearby, because who wants to take a chance driving around with a dead man?"

I gave him a look. "Sometimes I think you should have been a criminal."

"Back when I worked as a contractor, a lot of homeowners thought I was just that when they got the bill." He laughed, then backed the truck up until we were on the road again. "I'll tell you one thing, whoever shot Rory thought about this a little. He planned what he was doing. Not too much, or we'd probably never have found the body, but enough."

"Why him?" I asked. "Couldn't he have been a her?"

It was Mac's turn to give *me* a look. "*Now* who's the one thinking like a criminal?" he asked.

We drove back to the Cosden House. I made a phone call on the way to see if Iver Jones could meet with me. When we got to the project house, our homeowner's SUV was nowhere in sight, which was a relief. It was getting near three o'clock—a big chunk of another precious workday gone—so I left Mac to try to catch up on some work while I took a walk down to the Chesapeake City Historical Society to see Iver.

On the way, I thought about the fact that because the historical society owned the three-story brick hall with its fabulous view of the canal, as well as a spacious waterfront park next door. The organization was thus one of the wealthiest property owners in Chesapeake City. The historical society owned some of the best real estate in town. Location, location, location.

Very generously, their park was open to the public. A band shell there hosted weekly outdoor concerts in the summer, everything from blue grass to zydeco to blues. We hadn't been to a concert yet—and with any luck our project house would be done before the concert season kicked off. Weddings could be held in the park for a small fee.

And yet, for all its importance to the community, the prominent building was in a sad state of disrepair. The slate roof had loose or missing shingles. Whole sections of wooden soffit under the tall eaves were spongy with rot. Every last window needed to be reglazed and the sills dropped paint flakes into a bed of hostas below. As for the park itself, weeds sprouted among the beds and the plantings were a hodgepodge of spring bulbs, perennials and renegade violets. The park and the massive building that overlooked it were in need of a makeover. The kind that cost a lot of money. A wheelbarrow full of cash ought to do it. Trouble was, it looked to me as if the historical society didn't have enough cash to fill a coffee can.

I opened the door under the sign that read "Historical Society of Chesapeake City—Visitors Welcome" and entered a gloomy old hallway. My renovator's nose picked up the tell-tale smell of dampness. This building needed a dehumidifier and cross ventilation. I pushed open the door to the town museum.

Iver was ready for me—and he wasn't alone.

"It's about time you showed up here," said Iver, who had a way of making his words heavy with admonishment, as if I'd been holding up the progress of Western Civilization.

Sitting beside him was Maggie Delpino, who had the shop next door to Iver's. I hadn't seen Maggie since the day the body had turned up in the house. She looked different somehow. Maggie wore neo-hippie clothes and gaudy jewelry that she made herself and sold in her shop, The Magpie. Today, she had on a loose-fitting, tie-dye shirt that was sort of belted in the middle, a string of multi-colored metallic beads and earrings to match. No, her style hadn't changed. What was different about her? Then I realized what it was. Maggie was one of the most cheerful people I'd met in Canal Town, but she wasn't smiling now.

"I'm here as a witness," she informed me.

"A witness for what?"

"Just in case you attack poor Iver again."

"But it wasn't me!"

"Well, it's hard to know who to believe anymore, isn't it? This whole town has gone crazy." Maggie sniffed. She waved a canister in her right hand. "I've got my pepper spray right here, so don't try anything."

As I inched away from Maggie, I caught Iver's eye. "You know it wasn't me who pushed you down the stairs, Iver. You even told the police that. How are you feeling, anyhow?"

"Not bad for an old man," he said. "You could have visited me in the hospital, you know."

"I don't think the police would have liked that," I said. "In fact, I seem to recall that they warned me to stay away."

Iver nodded to concede the point. "What can I do for you today? If you've finally come around to visit, it must be because you want something."

I reached into my shirt pocket. The sudden motion must have upset Maggie, who raised the can of pepper spray threateningly. "Not so fast! What have you got in there, buster?

"Take it easy with that stuff," I said. "You might hurt somebody—like me."

Keeping one eye on Maggie, who had me dead to rights if she pressed the button on her nasty little canister, I handed Iver the delivery paperwork for the Sears house I had found at Rory's trailer.

"What's this?" he asked.

"That's what I was hoping you could tell me."

"It's got our stamp on it," he said. "Property of Chesapeake City Historical Society. But how did you get hold of it. Did you steal it?"

"No!" I said, glancing nervously again at the Annie Oakley of pepper spray sitting across from me. "We found it today at Rory Cosden's home. Look at the date."

Iver had a pair of reading glasses on a string around his neck, and he put them on to examine the document more closely. I noticed then that he had a bruise the size of an orange on his temple, as well as smaller bruises up and down his arms. The glasses had tape on them that indicated some sort of repair. I was pretty sure the tape hadn't been there the last time I had talked to him. Iver could be a difficult person to like, but that was no reason to push him down the stairs. Just thinking about it made me angry. No wonder Maggie couldn't wait to use her pepper spray on somebody.

"Why, it's a delivery receipt for a house!" Iver said, clearly surprised. He glanced at me over the tops of his battered reading glasses. "It's dated for the day—"

"—that Leo Cosden's ship went down. I know."

"But where on earth did it come from?"

"Deputy Sullivan took Mac and me over to Rory's house this afternoon. We found it there."

"But how did Rory get it?"

"Clearly, he took it from the historical society. He did do a lot of research here, didn't he?"

"Well, yes he did. Rory loved his local history, especially anything to do with his family, though he wasn't what you might call a scholar. I basically banned him months ago. He made such a mess—"

"Wouldn't someone have noticed this document earlier?" I asked.

"We stamp everything that comes in. People are always donating boxes of old papers that they find in the attic when they're cleaning out the house of an older relative who passed away. The last big batch we got came from Edith Cosden when she sold her father's house." He sounded sheepish for the first time. "But we don't really read everything that carefully, if that's what you mean."

"Could Rory have come across this bill of sale in that box of papers that Edith donated?"

"Yes, I suppose that's the only explanation." He shuffled through a handful of papers. "I'd say just about everyone in town has been through here at one time or another, looking for something to do with an ancestor or an old house."

"Iver, Rory must have found this document months ago and didn't know what to do with it," I said. "He must have wondered how in the world there was a delivery receipt signed by Leo Cosden on the day he died, when his ship sank later that day, taking Leo and his new Sears house with it. Rory must have realized there was more to the story. No wonder he was so damn grumpy all the time."

Iver nodded. "And then you found the body in the wall."

"Now the document made sense to Rory," I said. "But Captain Ezra Cosden was his hero. His great-grandfather. How could Ezra have come to possess a bill of sale that should have disappeared along with his brother's ship? Rory must have wrestled with the fact that maybe the captain had been a murderer."

Maggie spoke up. She had let go of the pepper spray and was looking over Iver's shoulder at the decades-old document. "And someone killed him." She shuddered. "It's like I don't even know the town where I live anymore."

I left the original document at the historical society, where it rightfully belonged. Iver made me a copy first. Then I took my leave of the two shop owners and walked the three blocks back to the Cosden House. From the street, the place looked a mess. There was a Dumpster out front piled high with construction debris. The shattered front window was covered with plywood. The whole exterior could have stood a new paint job—but we needed better weather first. A winter chill still clung to the air, though the calendar said it was spring. Altogether, the house looked more than a little careworn. I noticed a car I didn't recognize parked out front and frowned. Just our luck it would be a building inspector. We were due for one to come out and sign off on the plumbing before we closed up the bathroom walls upstairs. I sighed and marched dutifully toward the house, then climbed the steps to the front porch.

"Looks like you could use a little help with this house."

The voice startled me, though it was like hearing an angel. I hadn't seen her sitting there, in the half-broken porch swing. She looked sexy as ever, wearing a *Delmarva Renovators* sweat-shirt that hugged her body in all the right places. Absently, she flipped back her hair, then got to her feet, buckling on a tool belt as she stood.

Jenny Cooper had come back to work.

CHAPTER 17

"We need to talk," she said.

"Sure," I managed to reply, and moved to take a seat on a wobbly folding lawn chair that someone had salvaged from the trash. Or maybe it was just me that wobbled. I was more than a little stunned to see her again.

"Not now," Jenny said impatiently. "Later, all right? Right now we need to get moving on this house. From what I've seen, you haven't done much while I've been gone."

"You are kidding, right?" I was glad to see Jenny, but I couldn't help feeling defensive after that comment, as if she thought we couldn't fend for ourselves. "Let me catch you up on what's been happening around here. For starters, we found a body in the wall. Someone slashed our tires and threw a brick through the front window. Oh, did I mention I was this close to getting arrested on assault charges? And Rory Cosden is dead—murdered, it looks like."

"I know all that," Jenny snapped. "What I meant, Tom, is that there's a lot of work to be done around here."

I bit back any further excuses. Jenny was right—as usual. There was a lot of work to do on the Cosden House. Having Jenny back was a good start, but the truth was that we could have used an army of carpenters right about now. "Where do you want to begin?"

"You and Mac got the kitchen cabinets up, so I thought we

could work on the counter tops next. Try to get the kitchen done."

"I'll grab Iggy," I said. "We'll want video of this. And we'll need Mac. Those granite counter tops weigh about a ton."

I started to walk off, my thoughts already racing in a dozen different directions as I considered the project ahead. Did we have shims for the counters? Caulk for setting the sink? Kat might have to make a run for the hardware store—

"Tom?"

Jenny's tone yanked me back to the present. "Yeah?"

"It's good to be back," she said.

"And I'm glad you're here."

We pulled a marathon workday. Jenny's return gave our crew a burst of much-needed energy. She was our host, our star—call her what you wanted, but we all knew that we needed Jenny if this show was going to make it. Mac and I could muddle through on camera, doing our bit, but Jenny was the real reason people watched. Jenny got the job done with style. Viewers had even posted comments or e-mailed to say that they had never even picked up a hammer in their lives, but that Jenny was inspiring them to renovate. Some had actually gone out and purchased old houses—even inviting us to come out and film a session. If *Delmarva Renovators* was catching fire at all, it was because of Jenny Cooper.

Slowly, the realization began to sink in. *Jenny was back.* I was still too stunned by her return to know how I really felt about it. Walking back into the house, I tried to decide. Sure, I was glad she had decided to come back. But there were complications to work out. When Jenny promised that we would "talk later," I knew well enough that we'd be discussing what had happened between us. I suppose that like most guys, I'd prefer to cut off my leg with a dull saw than discuss relationships and feelings. Not that I was going to have any choice. I threw myself into the work to forget about all that, at least for a little while.

"Okay, everybody, let's get going." I clapped my hands together. "Lights, camera, action!"

Iggy rolled his eyes and grumbled just loud enough for me to hear "There he goes again, thinking he's John Ford."

First, we tackled the granite counter tops. Jenny worked her magic in the kitchen, but not the sort that involved pots and pans. The daylight was fading, so Kat set up lights and Iggy filmed while Jenny explained the finer points of granite counter tops. Despite my earlier fears, we had all the supplies on hand that we needed. These counter tops were real beauties, made of a dark, almost black granite that was flecked with clear grains of quartz in the same way that a good steak is marbled with fat. Flecks of gold sparked here and there—so-called "Fool's Gold," but dazzling as the real thing. These counter tops looked too good to eat off. You could have supplied a dozen kitchens with Formica counter tops for what this stuff cost, shipped all the way from Italy.

While Jenny finished up the counters, Mac and I moved on to a project that had been nagging at us, which was to put back the windows we had taken out to reglaze and paint. This was a time-consuming project, but with the house moving closer to completion it had to be done—if for no other reason than simple security. Up until now, we had been relying on the storm windows, but that wasn't enough anymore.

Mac and I walked down to the work area by the backyard shed—the one hiding the bathtub—and brought back a few refurbished windows. They were heavy, being solid wood and leaded glass, so we could carry just one at a time. Working together, we began reinstalling the windows.

"Good for another hundred years," Mac said, holding a window in place while I tied off the sash chord and stuffed the pig iron weight back into its pocket. When we finished, the window slid easily up and down. It was painstaking work, but neither of us complained. Of all the jobs an old house required, repairing windows was my favorite. There was something immensely satisfying in taking a mechanical system that had worked so well almost a century before and making it function like new again. This was the reason Mac and I loved old houses. They were built to last. I thought about the tin can feel of Rory Cosden's trailer and shuddered.

"Something wrong?" Mac asked.

"Nothing a pizza can't fix."

It was getting late, so we ordered enough pizza to feed our crew. A couple of the pies had extra cheese and pepperoni. As I bit into a slice, feeling a rivulet of grease run down my chin, I mused that there really ought to be a patron saint credited with inventing pizza. I'd been raised Catholic but had given up on going to church. Enough of my Sunday School lessons stuck with me to recall that there was a patron saint of carpenters. Saint Joseph. If the Catholics ever came up with a patron saint of pizza, I might reconsider getting right with the Pope.

We kept working until nearly ten. Most of the windows were done by then. Yawning, Cindy Pritchard finally called it quits and headed toward her SUV. She was spending the night in town. I watched her drive off, then beckoned Mac to join me. We backed the truck around to the shed behind the house where we had been stockpiling fixtures and other items taken from the house. Cindy's genuine antique bathtub was just inside the door. Mac and I tossed the tub—well, more like wrestled it—into the back of the truck. By tomorrow morning, the old tub would be far, far away—anything to keep it out of Cindy's sight before she decided that she wanted it back in her twenty-first century bathroom.

Jenny knocked on my door just after midnight.

"You."

"Me?"

"It's time for that talk."

She pushed past me into the room without an invitation. Truth be told, I had been so busy the last few days that the room was kind of a mess. Room service made the bed and cleaned the bathroom, and the good maids at the Hampton Inn fluffed the pillows but stopped short of picking my dirty socks off the floor or neatening my work table, which was scattered now with notes and paperwork. Even in the digital age, there was no escaping the pen and paper. My laptop was open to the back end of our site, where I was busy updating our daily progress blog. My boys had been up late and I had spent a lot of time messaging them in between working on the blog.

Jenny didn't comment on the mess, but plunked down on the bed, which was relatively clear. Chastely, I scuttled back down into my office chair. A few weeks ago, I had swapped out the standard-issue hotel chair for a comfy upholstered version from the nearest office supply store.

"The killer always returns to the scene of the crime," Jenny said.

"Excuse me?" I jolted upright in my chair, the memory of Rory's submerged pickup truck fresh in my mind.

"You know," she said, smoothing the bed spread pointedly.

"Oh," I said. "Whew. For a minute there I thought you were talking about Rory's death."

"No, Tom, I'm talking about us. What happened between us."

"I'm sorry about that," I began. Jenny had given me fair warning that we'd be having this talk. In the back of my mind, almost subliminally, I had been coming up alternately with lines of defense or sincere apologies in between hanging sash weights. "I never meant to hurt you or the show."

"Sorry?" Jenny shook her head. "You have nothing to be sorry about."

All of a sudden I felt like a dog that had been expecting to be whipped, but that had been thrown a biscuit instead. "I don't?" I said tentatively. I revisited all those lines I had been practicing and watched them evaporate. Old houses I could figure out. Women, on the other hand . . .

"When you think about it, it's a lot like sleeping with my

brother," she said.

"You slept with your brother?"

"I'm being metaphorical here," she said. "We did practice French kissing once, which was pretty gross, now that I think about it. Anyhow, Tom, what I'm trying to say is that we're two lonely people."

"We are?"

"You're separated from your wife. You miss your sons. My God. I'm pretty much a loner, living out of a suitcase in a motel room."

"When you put it that way—"

"What happened between us wasn't sordid, Tom. It was beautiful. A gift between two lonely people."

"Then why does it feel so icky?"

"Icky?"

"You know. Weird. Uncomfortable."

"Because it's a sign that it shouldn't happen again," Jenny said.

In my alternate universe, Jenny and I would already have our clothes off, feeling the smooth slide of flesh on flesh, that business about the inappropriateness of the situation be damned. Just thinking about it, I felt myself getting worked up.

But I knew I was right. Having sex again with Jenny would be icky. So what I did was walk over and give Jenny a peck on the cheek.

She stood up and it looked like there was something she wanted to say.

"What?"

"Nothing. Good night, Tom."

The door closed behind her. Everything was going to be all right between us. It seemed a little too easy, as a matter of fact. Jenny must have thought the same thing. Because I was pretty sure that out in the hallway, I heard the sound of a muffled sob.

CHAPTER 18

The next morning, Carl Batzer stood poised with the coffee pot hovering over my mug but chose first to fill my ears with gossip. "People are saying maybe it was a jealous husband," he remarked, not without a certain amount of relish.

"What are you talking about?" I'd spent most of the night tossing and turning as my thoughts took turns churning over Jenny, then the house, and finally the murder. "Pour the coffee, Carl. I need caffeine to think straight."

"Grumpy, huh? This ought to help. Strongest coffee on the Eastern Shore." He grinned as he filled my mug. "It was in the paper this morning that Rory was shot. It's all over town that maybe he was fooling around with somebody's wife."

"Rory?" I asked in disbelief. Rory was many things, but it was doubtful that Lothario was on his resume. Don Juan he hadn't been.

"Why else would someone shoot him?" Carl asked. "Maybe he was carrying on with that woman you're fixing up the house for. That one's got round heels, if you ask me."

Carl winked and moved on to the next customer on my left, Pete Morrison. He shook his head.

"No more for me," he said. "Too much of that stuff makes my hands shake and I can't paint worth a damn."

I took my first gulp of the viscous coffee and nearly choked. As Carl had promised, it was strong. Maybe even strong enough to dissolve the enamel in the mug, or melt spoons. Damn, but it was good. I took another gulp and felt the morning fog in my head being blown away by a gale force caffeinated wind.

I turned to Mac, who was busy attacking his bacon and eggs. "What are round heels?"

"You're asking the wrong guy," he mumbled around a mouthful of food. He washed it down with a noisy slurp of coffee. "I don't know anything about fashion."

"Never mind."

I looked around the café. Carl's place had atmosphere in the literal sense, a sort of greasy haze that hung in the air because the exhaust vents over the griddle couldn't keep pace with the huge amounts of bacon, eggs and French toast being cooked up for the hungry breakfast crowd. That greasy smoke permeated one's clothes so that you'd still be smelling like the café until at least lunchtime. I appreciated the effort that went into this sort of home cooking. With a pang, I thought of weekends with my boys, when I loved to make them a big breakfast. My wife liked to sleep in, and much to her annoyance she would wake to find that I had managed to get every dish and frying pan in the house dirty. I realized it had been too long since I had seen my boys. Phone calls and e-mail weren't the same. Once this old house project was finished, I planned on spending some quality time with them. Maybe we'd go camping, or head down to the beach for a long weekend.

Carl's daughter scooted past with a plate stacked high with pancakes and sausage, a big scoop of butter melting on the side. No one would have thought to call her a "server"—she would have taken offense. If you called her anything, it had better be "Hon." Carl served good, honest food—the coffee was an example—and lots of it. When you ate breakfast here, you wouldn't leave hungry and your wallet wouldn't take a huge hit.

Somewhere in the back of my mind, it registered that our show could have done so much with the café. Why would we want to change anything? The floor covering was red-and-white linoleum squares that had surely welcomed every sort of footwear seen in the past forty years. Mac and I had been there often enough that we now had our own unofficial stools at the counter, but the rest of the diners sat in wooden booths around the room. The booths had been built with sturdiness rather than comfort in mind—there was no padding on the benches, which encouraged good posture while discouraging leisurely meals. The other members of our crew were squeezed into one of these booths, where Jenny seemed to be holding court as various town residents stopped by to welcome her back. Just further proof that she was our only real star.

This morning, however, even Jenny was playing second fiddle to the real news. Newspaper pages flapped at almost every booth, while a few tech-savvy diners peered into their wireless devices as they read the news. *The Cecil Guardian* had broken the story that Rory Cosden had died from a gunshot wound and everybody was talking about it.

Carl was back to refill my coffee cup. "You should have been in here yesterday," he said, noticing me taking in the discussions around the room. "Rory's death was shocking, like somebody tossed a hand grenade in here. The news that he'd been shot exploded like an atom bomb."

Carl ran through his explosive superlatives too quickly, because what happened next was even bigger than an atom bomb. It was more like a supernova.

People saw her coming across the street and stopped what they were doing to stare. All over the café, forks paused in mid-air. It wasn't just because Sarah Cosden rarely came into the café or any other establishment that accepted money. She was famously stingy and preferred tea and toast at home to a big plate of Carl's scrambled eggs and hash browns. No, it was because if you looked up "Crazy Woman" in an illustrated dictionary, you would have seen her picture as a definition.

Sarah wore a bathrobe that once upon a time might have been canary yellow but had since faded to a dingy nicotine color. Her pale but shapely legs were bare as if she had slipped the robe on over not much of anything. Sarah was not a bad looking woman, and normally the thought of her naked would not have been unpleasant. But this morning it only added to her aura of madness. She stomped across the street in bright blue fuzzy slippers. She had serious bed-head, so that all her brownish hair perched to one side, the clump of hair looking for all the world like a muskrat clinging to her scalp. She paused just outside the door, the same way a thunderstorm will build on the horizon, then burst into the café.

"I know you've all heard the news by now that my cousin Rory was shot," she shouted. Her eyes stabbed around the room. "Murdered! You all have got your theories, I know. Well, I can tell you one thing. You're wrong! Every damn last one of you!"

Since it was his establishment, Carl stepped forward to bring some order to the café. "Now, Sarah—"

"Quiet!" she boomed. "I'm not done yet, Carl. I came in here to tell you people who killed Rory, and that's what I'm gonna do."

Carl retreated behind the counter. "All right," he said, not that Sarah was asking for his permission.

"It wasn't just one person, neither," she said. An accusing finger shot out and pointed in my direction. "You! Wrecking our grandpa's house the way you have, ruining his memory, and putting it on the computer for everybody to see. It's just wrong! It made Rory so upset."

I would have been less surprised if Sarah had opened her robe and flashed me. "You're saying we killed Rory? Our show?"

Out came that accusing pointing finger again. "There was no respect for what come before! You even got rid of the bathtub. It upsets me. I know it upset Rory. Digging up the past that's better left alone. Someone didn't like it."

"I thought we were so done with that bathtub," Mac muttered.

But I was more interested in what Sarah Cosden had to say. "Then who are you saying killed your cousin?"

"I know who did it. It will all come out in time, you just wait and see. You be sure and ask Iver about the money."

Then Sarah seemed to deflate, like a thundercloud that all the rain has gone out of. She clutched the robe more tightly around her, turned on her heel and slammed back out the door. Several diners craned their necks to follow her progress back across the street and down the sidewalk toward the old house on Bohemia Avenue she shared with her mother.

The quiet that followed Sarah's departure did not last. Everyone started talking at once over their now-cold plates of eggs. Because unless I was mistaken, she had just accused Iver Jones of murder.

"What are round heels?" I asked Jenny on the short drive from the café to the Cosden House.

She laughed. "I haven't heard that one in a while. It's an expression my grandmother used."

"What does it mean?"

"I don't think I'm going to tell you," she said, a playful smile on her lips. "You'll just have to find out on your own."

"Come on!"

"Nope."

As we pulled up in front of the house, Jenny grabbed her tool belt and slid off the seat. We had another long list of projects to tackle today. There were finishing touches to make in the kitchen, plus we had to finish framing in a bedroom closet that our homeowners had decided to add late in the game.

I was just walking into the house when Sully drove up in her cruiser.

"Well, well. I see you've decided to do some work today."

"As much as we like this town, we can't stay here forever."

"I heard about the scene down at the café," she said.

"Sounds like Sarah flipped her lid."

"You could say that. She also made some serious accusations about Iver."

"I'm not surprised."

"What do you mean?" I asked.

"Rory's will," she said. "The sole beneficiary of his life insurance policy was the historical society."

"They could use the money," I said. "That building needs a lot of work."

"It's got people talking. Sarah Cosden isn't the only one who is wondering about the will." Sully stood on the sidewalk out front, contemplating the house. "When are you putting the shutters back up?"

"That's the least of our worries right now. Listen, I've got a question for you. What does it mean when someone says a woman has round heels?"

"Don't tell him!" came a shout from inside the house. Jenny came out on the porch. I introduced her to Sully. I could see the two of them sizing each other up. We chatted politely for a few minutes, and then Sully said she had to get back to work. As she drove off in the police cruiser, Jenny stared after the car and said with a sniff: "Hmm. Bet that one's got round heels."

"Round. . . . oh. I think I get it now." I had to laugh. "Why, Jenny, that's the cattiest thing I've ever heard you say."

"Meow," she said.

After lunch, I went to see Maggie Delpino, who seemed to be the only person in Canal Town who hadn't heard the latest news about Rory Cosden.

"Shot?" Maggie put a hand to her chest in alarm. "Oh my goodness. Shot? Who would do such a thing?"

"Good question," I said. "That's what the police are trying to figure out right now. From what I understand, the list of suspects keeps getting longer."

"Oh my. I think I'd better sit down."

Maggie sank onto a stool behind the cluttered counter in her shop, The Magpie. The shop occupied the first floor of the old Sawtell's Drug Store building, while Maggie lived above the store. She had chosen the name of the shop well, considering that those namesake birds were known for seeking out shiny objects and then hoarding them in their nests. Maggie's shop was filled with just the sort of baubles that would have pleased a magpie—glittering necklaces and beaded bracelets, wind chimes, seashell-covered picture frames and hand-made jewelry. The shiny things were scattered among shelves filled with Chesapeake City T-shirts and sweatshirts, coffee mugs, postcards and books on local history. It all smelled really good, thanks to all the scented candles for sale.

"I can't believe you haven't heard the news," I said. "It was in the paper this morning. Everyone is talking about it."

"I haven't been out this morning and I don't get the paper," she said.

"I thought everyone around here read the Guardian."

She shook her head. "Too much negative energy from reading a newspaper. Who needs that? I don't. If anything really important happens, I hear about it." I might have pointed out that she hadn't heard about Rory being shot dead, but I kept my mouth shut. Maggie continued, "You see, I'm something of a Luddite. I don't have a cell phone or a computer. I don't have cable TV. I read instead. I send letters. I use a typewriter when I want to get fancy. And I don't accept credit cards." She tapped a hand-lettered sign on her counter that read, "CASH OR CHECK ONLY PLEASE."

"Doesn't that limit your business?" I wondered.

"There's business," Maggie sniffed, then put a little steel into her voice. "And then there are principles."

I reconsidered Maggie now, as if seeing her for the first time. I'd always taken her for one of those artsy, impractical people—just the sort of person who eeked out a living running a shop called The Magpie in a touristy waterfront village. She was neither frumpy nor unattractive. Quite the opposite. Mag-

gie had a style all her own. She wore flowing clothes with colorful designs, glasses with fashionably clunky frames, old-
school high-top sneakers with bright socks. Her raven hair was
pulled back into a business-like ponytail. At first glance, Maggie
left a youthful impression. But she had the beginnings of
crow's feet at the corners of her eyes and smile lines around
her mouth. Late forties or maybe fifty at the most. As far as I
knew, Maggie was single and unattached, a fact that would not
have gone unnoticed in town.

"One theory that's going around town is that Rory was
something of a ladies' man," I said. "Carl Batzer down at the
café says there's a rumor that Rory was shot by a jealous
husband. What do you think about that?"

Now I felt Maggie looking me over as if she was recon-
sidering *me*. "It seems to me, Mr. Martell, that you are playing
detective." She gave me a smile that wasn't altogether warm. "I
thought you would have had enough to keep you busy down at
the Cosden House."

"You know that expression, 'If these walls could talk . . .'?
Let's just say the Cosden House has a lot to say."

"Mmm. Well, I haven't heard about any goings-on with
Rory. Nothing out of the ordinary, at least."

"Out of the ordinary? That means you *have* heard something."

"Rory was an eligible bachelor," Maggie said. "Not my kind,
mind you, but I'm sure he was *somebody's* kind. You haven't
been here long enough to get involved in it, but there's quite a
dating scene here in town. There are a lot of single people here.
Lonely people. The waterfront, the old-time streets, the atmosphere here, it draws people looking for a fresh start after a
divorce or maybe just a tough life that hasn't worked out all
that well somewhere else. Take me, for instance. I was married
for twenty years and had a career as an accountant. I have a
lovely daughter away at college. Before the divorce, we had a
big mortgage on a vinyl-sided McMansion in a development
outside Baltimore. Now I'm here. Now I can be me and live

the life I want."

"I guess not everything is what it seems."

"You were oblivious to it—men usually are—but there was quite a bit of speculation about you when you showed up in town. What's the expression?" She grinned. "Fresh meat."

"Oh?"

"There were women—and a few men—who wondered if you were available. Maureen Sullivan was one of them."

"Deputy Sullivan?"

"She asked around about you—and then your friend Mac— in a way that wasn't entirely related to law enforcement."

"What did you say?"

"Oh . . . well . . . you know," Maggie replied with a smile that indicated that was all she was going to say on the subject.

I guess I still had a lot more to learn about small towns. So maybe Carl Batzer hadn't been entirely off base with his speculation that Rory got shot for messing around with the wrong woman. But there was something else I wanted to ask Maggie about.

"This morning at the café, Sarah Cosden marched in like she was storming the Bastille and announced that Iver Jones had something to do with her cousin's murder."

"Iver?" Maggie's eyebrows went up, and then she started to laugh. "As if anyone could actually think that Iver was capable of shooting anyone. It would be more his style to talk them to death."

"I heard from a reliable source that the historical society is going to inherit money from Rory's estate. The historical society is the one and only beneficiary."

Maggie fidgeted with a box of polished stones on her counter. "As a matter of fact, that does happen to be true, as far as I know."

"How much money are we talking about?"

"Well, Rory didn't have much in his bank account, but I understand that he did have a life insurance policy, so I guess it could be as much as a couple hundred thousand dollars."

"Oh." It was true that at first glance, Rory must not have had much money. I had seen the modest trailer where he lived. But I hadn't considered insurance money. Suddenly, I was seeing things in a whole new light.

"He wouldn't have," Maggie said, as if reading my mind.

"Wouldn't have what?" I asked.

But Maggie didn't get a chance to answer. Some customers came in, a retired couple, and Maggie took that as an excuse to run out from behind the counter and hover over them. That was okay. I didn't need to hear more. A couple hundred thousand? People had been murdered over a whole lot less.

CHAPTER 19

Peaceful. At first glance, that was how the swimmer in the town harbor looked, drifting on the surface of the still water. Iver Jones watched from the shoreline. He was out early, tending the garden around Franklin Hall, when he happened to notice the swimmer. Iver didn't pay much attention at first, although it was unusual to see someone in the water. It was awfully early, with clumps of morning mist still drifting across the still surface of the harbor. Not many people went swimming in the harbor. In fact, if Iver recalled correctly, the town had even passed some kind of ordinance against it. It was never actually enforced. Some boater or teenagers were always jumping in on hot days. And on Canal Day the harbor had more bikinis in it than the set of Beach Blanket Bingo.

Iver stooped to attack a stubborn clump of violets coming up between his chocolate iris plants. The violets in this garden would take over if he turned his back on them for so much as a minute. They were comely enough in their own way when they bloomed, tiny bursts of purple, but Iver stuck to the old gardener's adage that a weed was simply a plant out of place, no matter how pretty. So he tugged and pulled at the violets, working up a sweat. At his age, gardening was excellent exercise.

When he straightened up a minute later, panting a bit from his efforts, he happened to look out again at the swimmer. It was clear now that something was wrong. The figure now bumped against the hull of a moored sailboat like a piece of driftwood. Then the slight current in the harbor carried the person closer to shore.

He saw now that the body was face-down in the water. The person wore a dress that fanned out in the current. It was an old-fashioned dress, he thought. Her long hair twisted and twitched as if it were trying to stay afloat of its own accord. There was something oddly familiar about the body. He was sure he would know the person, if only he could see her face.

Iver was normally a calm person in what he liked to call "situations." Not much fazed him, not the occasional shop-lifter in his shop, not even being shoved down the stairs at the historical society. But this situation—a body in the harbor— was out of the ordinary. He considered what to do. He didn't have a cell phone. It was a long walk back around the building, then up the stairs to the second-floor office of the historical society. Just thinking about it, he felt his old bones ache.

He stared for another minute, knowing that the person out there was beyond help, and then Iver took a deep breath and started shouting for help.

I was up on a ladder, wiring in a ceiling fan, when Kat came through the door.

"Whoa. What's the rush?"

"Somebody else died," she panted. "I thought you'd want to know right away."

"Who?"

"I don't know. The fire company is down there now, getting the body out of the harbor."

I left the fan half-wired, hanging by its mounting hook, and got down off the ladder. Vaguely, I remembered the fire whistle going off three times, which meant a fire or an ac-cident. Mac was making a supply run and Marsha was out with the homeowner shopping for fabric—I'm sure that meant she was in heaven right about now—so I left Iggy to mind the house and headed out with Kat.

Half the town was down at the waterfront. The fire company rescue boat was out, but apparently it was too late to save anyone.

"Drowned," remarked Carl Batzer, who had come right from the café, still wearing an apron.

"Who?"

"Some of the firefighters are saying it's Sarah Cosden."

"Oh my God," said Kat, who had come down to the waterfront with me. "The crazy lady from breakfast yesterday?"

"You wouldn't be far wrong about that, Missy," Carl said. "Who else goes swimming in the town harbor wearing a dress except a crazy person?"

"Unless she meant to drown herself," Kat pointed out. "Suicide."

It did seem like the obvious thing, but then I thought of Rory Cosden's truck in Back Creek. That had also seemed like suicide at first. But people didn't normally shoot themselves in the chest and then navigate their pickup trucks through an obstacle course of guardrails, marsh and scrub trees to reach a creek. Someone had wanted to make Rory's death appear to be a suicide. Had they done the same to Sarah Cosden. But who? And why?

Carl seemed to be mulling over the same question. I could almost see the gears churning inside his head. "Suicide, huh? Then why not just jump off the bridge? If you wanted to kill yourself, that would be quick and easy."

"I'm really not sure that people intent on killing themselves are in the right frame of mind to do much planning," I pointed out. Though I had to admit that a swan dive off the soaring steel arch of the bridge more than two hundred feet above the canal would most certainly be fatal.

"Have people jumped off the bridge before?" Kat asked.

"Well, sure. The last time was back in ninety-two." Carl winked. "Back before you were born, Missy."

"I was so born," Kat said defensively—never mind that she was still in diapers. "What happened?"

"The poor fellow climbed to the top of the arch and then maybe sobered up or chickened out. Most of the town came out to watch. It was quite a show. In the end, it looked like maybe he lost his balance and fell."

"Oh." Kat looked a little pale.

"All right, Carl. Stop scaring my crew. Don't you have any customers?"

"They're all down here."

"Kat, why don't you head back to the house? I'll see you there."

She nodded. "Good idea."

Kat headed off, and I wandered the harborfront looking for familiar faces. Out on the water, the fire company boat had already retrieved the body, and was motoring back to the boat launch on the opposite side of the harbor from the town dock. I could see an ambulance waiting over there. The townspeople watched the boat's slow progress with expressions of horrified fascination. Wandering along, I picked up snatches of information. Everyone was talking about the dress Sarah had been wearing. Several people had seen the firefighters pull the body from the water, and they said Sarah had on a flowing, old-fashioned gown, almost like a wedding dress. Someone told a friend about the scene Sarah had made yesterday at the café, while someone else revealed that Iver Jones had been the first to spot the body.

I glimpsed Sully, out of uniform, but once again wearing her blue nylon windbreaker with CCSO across the back in big yellow letters. She carried a walkie talkie and was keeping people from crowding too close to the edge of the city dock. One drowning was plenty enough.

"We've really got to stop meeting like this," I said, a little of the gallows humor from my police reporter days slipping out. I couldn't help myself. "What happened?"

"You know as much as I do," Sully said. "Looks like she

drowned."

"First Rory Cosden, now his cousin," I said. "You've got to admit, this seems strange. Yesterday in the diner, she announced that she knew who killed Rory. If it wasn't an accident, maybe someone was trying to shut her up."

Sully motioned for me to follow her. We walked a few feet away, out of earshot of the crowd. Looking back at the people gathered to watch the recovery operation, I could see that this was a real tragedy for the town. Rory and Sarah had not been prominent or even particularly well-liked, but the people gathered here had grown up with them, gone to school and church with them, had even done the same with Rory and Sarah's parents and grandparents in some cases. They might not have loved Rory and Sarah, but they had been two of Chesapeake City's own. They were Cosdens, after all. A palpable sense of loss seemed to hang over the crowd.

Sully spoke in a hushed tone. "The medical examiner is going to do a toxicology report," she explained. "He'll be looking for drugs or alcohol in Sarah's system. That could help explain her mental state—either suicide or impaired judgment in deciding to go for a swim."

I gave her a doubtful look. "Maybe. You know that Sarah announced yesterday morning at the café that she knew who killed Rory."

"I heard."

"What if someone was trying to keep her quiet?"

Sully cast a glance at the crowd. Was it just my imagination, or were two or three people looking our way with more than idle curiosity? "You better keep that thought to yourself. Having theories about why someone was killed and who killed them could be dangerous right now."

"What happens now?" I asked.

"The toxicology report—"

"I know that," I said hurriedly. "What I mean is, what are we going to do?"

"What do you mean 'we'?" she asked. "I'm the deputy.

You're the renovator. Try to remember that."

"I seem to recall you asking us to help out with Rory Cosden's house," I said. "Or did you forget that already?"

"Nobody is going snooping around Sarah's place, if that's what you're getting at," Sully said. "She lived with her mother, so we can't just go barging in, especially not if there's no reason to do so."

"Let me know if you find anything," I said. "I really need to get back to the house."

"All right," Sully said. As I started to walk away, she called me back. "Do me a favor, Tom. Make sure you keep any eye out for yourself and your crew. I wouldn't have said Rory and Sarah were particularly close, but they did have one thing in common with each other—and with you."

I nodded. "The Cosden House."

"It could be a coincidence, but you never know," Deputy Sullivan said. "So do me a favor and be careful."

I called Mac. He explained that he was in the checkout line at what was euphemistically known as a Home Center—a massive box of a building with every tool and gadget a renovator could possibly need. Religious people had church, art lovers had museums, and do-it-yourselfers had the aisles at their local home center where they could wander and daydream about their next project. The nearest one was several miles from Canal Town—in another state, as a matter of fact—but we needed a few supplies at the house and the low prices made it worth the trip.

"Sully already called me with the news," he said.

"Oh." That caused me to raise an eyebrow on my end of the line. Mac and Sully were getting along better than I had guessed—the deputy hadn't called me with any inside information. Something in my voice must have given me away.

"I hope you're not getting jealous on me," Mac said. In the background, I could hear the scanner beeping as it rang up purchases. "Don't forget, you're the one who slept with Jenny, not me. One woman at a time, Hammer. That means I've got dibs on Sully."

"I wouldn't have it any other way," I said, trying to sound genuine. In the back of my mind, I wondered what Sully would say to the notion of anyone having dibs on her. "I hope it works out for you two."

The beeping got louder. "Okay, I'm about to check out here. What do you think about Sarah Cosden? Suicide or something else? Just in case anyone is keeping count, that's two Cosdens gone in as many days."

"Mac, you're the one who told me the first rule of police work."

"Yeah, there's no such thing as coincidence. Gotta go." Mac hung up.

I know I had plenty of work to do. I had an old house to renovate, not to mention a show to run. But now I was just plain curious. And Chesapeake City was a small town. So I did what several townspeople were already doing, which was to hang out in front of Sarah and Edith Cosdens' house.

Nobody wanted to be too obvious about it, so the way to handle this was to sit on someone's front porch where you could keep an eye on their house. The Cosdens lived on Bohemia Avenue, in a house that had been cut up into apartments. I joined a group of people who had occupied the rocking chairs and porch steps of the house across the street. Ostensibly, we were just chewing the fat about the news in town, but in reality we wanted to keep an eye on what was going on across the way. We didn't have to wait long before a couple of deputies pulled up in front of the Cosdens'. One of them was Sully, the other was a plainclothes detective I didn't recognize. Another car drove up, and a man wearing a minister's black shirt and collar followed the deputies in. No more than twenty minutes later, Sully came back out carrying something that I recognized from police shows as being an evidence bag.

I got up and crossed the street. If it had just been any cop, I wouldn't have done it. But I felt like I knew Sully well enough at this point to be nosy. I also knew her well enough to see that she looked sad.

"What did you find?" I asked.

Sully held up the evidence bag. It held a pistol. Nothing at all like the modern Glock that she carried. No, this was an antique weapon, like you might see stuck into the belt of a Revolutionary War soldier. Just the kind of pistol that fired a musket ball like the one that had killed Rory.

"We also found a suicide note," Sully said. "It was typed on Sarah's computer and printed out. She admitted shooting Rory. She said it was because he had stolen some of the Cosden family heirlooms for that mini-museum of his and wouldn't give them back. She wrote that she killed herself because she was distraught about shooting her cousin."

"That's awful."

"It's sad to think that some people in this town are so stuck in the past that they would kill over it." Sully sighed, then opened the trunk of her cruiser and put in the evidence bag. "Anyhow, I guess that means the mystery is solved. We know who shot Rory, and we know why Sarah ended up in the harbor."

I wasn't so sure. It all seemed a little too neat to me. Rory leaving an envelope with my name on it, for instance. At the café yesterday morning, Sarah had made a public announcement that she knew the identity of Rory's killer. Was she really talking about herself? Sully seemed satisfied about the explanation for the two recent deaths. But what about the death that had taken place long before, back in 1913? Most of us had gotten so caught up in recent events that we had nearly forgotten about our mummified friend who had been entombed in the wall. However, it was doubtful that the Cosden family had forgotten, and I was pretty sure the body in the wall had

something to do with the events of the past two days. The
question was, how many more bodies were going to turn up?

CHAPTER 20

Iver Jones was having a cup of tea in the office of the historical society. It was finally warming up outside and shaping up to be another fine spring day. The morning mist had lingered longer than usual but was finally burning off as the sun made an appearance. In the glaring light, the scene earlier that day at the town harbor now all seemed like a bad dream. But inside Franklin Hall it was still cold and damp, the old bricks and lumber hanging on to winter's chill. Iver pulled on a nylon windbreaker and he cradled a mug of tea in his hands, absorbing its warmth.

"How are you doing?" I asked.

"As well as can be expected," he replied. He didn't add the second part of his sentence, *for having seen a drowned body this morning.* At first, when I'd heard that Iver had been the one to find Sarah's body, I had to admit that I'd been suspicious. But then I learned of the circumstances involved. Iver had been gardening, and Sarah's body was found floating far from shore. Given the logistics involved, it was unlikely that Iver had anything to do with Sarah's departure from this world. Still, it seemed an odd coincidence. I'd also been surprised when I found Iver alone. Why had he let his guard down? At one point I'd been accused of pushing him down the stairs—but Iver must have been convinced now that it hadn't been me.

"Can I do anything for you?"

Iver shook his head. "Oh, I'll be fine. A cup of tea is just what the doctor ordered. Anyhow, I'm doing a lot better than that poor Sarah Cosden."

"Iver, you know more about town history than just about anybody else," I said. "What in the world is going on?"

"It's already around town that Sarah left a suicide note," he said. "The note explained that she killed Rory."

"Shot him with an antique pistol," I elaborated. "I saw the police take it out of her place."

"Yes."

"I think there's more going on here." I looked pointedly at Iver. "Maybe this has something to do with Leo Cosden. What was going on back then, Iver? We know there must have been a terrible rivalry between the two brothers, Leo and Ezra. But I don't think you're telling me the whole story."

Iver sipped his tea and shifted uncomfortably. "I've been doing a little research since this whole business started. I can tell you something I found out, something particularly sad, which is that by all accounts Leo and Ezra were inseparable as boys. Brothers, but also best friends. They did everything together. Pick on one, and you had the other to deal with as well. It's also likely that they were always competing against each other in the way boys do. Who could swim the fastest across the canal, that sort of thing. When they grew up and competed in the shipping trade, it became something more than sibling rivalry. Something more bitter and ugly."

"Ah." I paused. "Here's what I know so far about what happened back in 1913. Leo Cosden tried to outrun the storm and sail home from Baltimore, but his ship was caught in the heart of the nor'easter. He was bringing back a Sears Roebuck house that he planned to build here in town. But the house went down with the ship. What was his hurry, Iver? Why was he so eager to build a house?"

Iver sipped his tea. "There may have been a woman involved."

Now the story was starting to make more sense. "Leo's ship

would have made a lot of trips to Baltimore . . ."

"I think he had a flame there." Iver smiled knowingly over the rim of his mug as he warmed to the subject. The man really loved to dish. "More than a flame. After Leo disappeared, a woman arrived on the Ericcson Line steamer, claiming that she carried the captain's baby."

I could only stare. "How do you know all this?"

"Edith Cosden told me the story, years ago. It was the sort of thing, she said, that children overhear adults whispering about when they don't think the children can understand. But children understand more than they let on. She told me that the woman was turned away. Ezra Cosden had inherited his brother's property and his other ships by then. His brother's death had made him wealthy. He wanted nothing to do with his dead brother's woman. What if she made some sort of claim to Leo's property? It might have cost Ezra money, you see. Eventually, she left town."

"I think I'll have that cup of tea now," I said, reaching for the electric pot. Iver handed me a mug with a tea bag in it, and I poured hot water over it. I declined his offer of milk, sugar or lemon. While the tea steeped, I tried to imagine what it must have been like for a young, unwed mother in 1913. Society had a different moral standard in those days. People were inclined to be even more judgmental then. Unless a woman had a supportive family or money of her own, it was likely that Leo Cosden's lover and child had faced a difficult future. That was all in the past now. I wondered how their lives had turned out. I looked at Iver. "What happened?"

"Who knows? Edith didn't. I think that as she grew older, she felt bad for that woman and her baby. The baby would have been a Cosden, after all, if not in name then by blood. Edith also had a theory."

"Go on."

"Apparently, Leo had a flair for dramatics. He was also secretive, like his brother Ezra. They kept their business to themselves. Edith always wondered if Leo had planned to build the Sears house, then bring his new bride home to live in it. Imagine how that would have surprised the town and impressed his new wife! But the storm—and the baby—weren't part of the plan."

I gulped the tea, nearly scalding the roof of my mouth in the process. "That's an amazing story," I said.

"Just a story," Iver reminded me. "But sometimes with history, you have to make an educated guess and use a little imagination to fill in the blanks. And what if it did happen that way? Maybe one cousin wanted the truth to come out, and the other didn't."

"Would it be worth killing to cover up the past?"

Iver sniffed. "When it comes to the Cosdens, I'd say the past has a way of getting mixed up with the present."

When I got back to the house, Mac was busy unloading some of the supplies he'd bought at the home center. Adhesive, tubes of caulk, drywall screws, plastic plumber's shims. Old houses devoured those things the way a bear ate honey.

"Where have you been, Hammer?" he asked. "You do remember that we have a house to work on here, right?"

"Do we still have that big magnet out in the shed?"

"Yeah, I think so. Why?"

"Do you mind seeing if you can find it? I'll go dig up some rope."

"Uh-oh. I don't like the sound of this. Did you drop something down the old well?"

"No."

"Then please tell me this has something to do with the house."

"Believe me, it has everything to do with the house."

Mac was back in a few minutes with the magnet. We had picked it up at a yard sale in town. Along with old anchors and oars, crab pots and buoys, it was just the sort of thing one might find at a yard sale in a waterfront town. The magnet was about the size of a dinner plate, with a big ring in the back of it for securing a rope. It was an underwater retrieval magnet, which came in handy when you dropped your tools in the water while working on a dock or a boat. The magnet was powerful enough to pick up a hammer.

We hopped in the truck, and I explained my theory to Mac.

"So what you're saying is, the police didn't dredge the creek for a murder weapon, so it must still be in the bottom of the creek." Mac shook his head. "I don't know. They found the pistol used to kill Rory at Sarah Cosden's house."

"Humor me," I said.

"Sounds like I haven't got a choice."

We parked on the shoulder of the road and walked out on the bridge. I'd brought along a section of two-by-four for demonstration purposes. "Now, let's say you shot Rory and just finished driving his truck into the creek. You come out on the bridge to examine your handiwork. Pretty good job. Rory is dead. The truck is mostly submerged. You still have the pistol in your pocket. You toss it into the water." I handed him the wood. "Try it."

The two-by-four hit the water about fifteen feet from the bridge. The wood did not sink, and the current was swift enough to carry it back toward us. But the main point of the exercise had been to show us approximately where a pistol would have gone into the water.

"Now what?"

"Now we go fishing." I lowered the magnet at the end of the rope into the water until it hit bottom. The impact was soft, so I assumed I'd struck mud. I hauled in the rope to raise the magnet and tried again a few feet over. This time, something felt different. Slowly, I pulled in the rope, hand over hand. An object covered in muck was stuck to the magnet.

Mack pulled it free and shook off enough mud to reveal a set of bicycle handlebars. "Congratulations. This could be the murder weapon, all right—if Rory had been beaten to death with a Schwinn."

"Very funny. Let's try again." I dropped the magnet back into the water.

"This shouldn't take long," Mac commented. "Heck, there must only be several hundred square feet of water within throwing distance and our magnet is, what, about one square foot?"

My next catch was a hubcab. Followed by a rusty fishing pole that someone must have lost long ago. And then something came up from the mud that wasn't nearly as corroded or as covered in goop as the other items had been. I could tell what it was as soon as it broke free of the creek.

"Good Lord, Hammer, is that what I think it is?"

Because what I'd pulled from the creek was an antique pistol that was the twin of the weapon that the police had found in Sarah Cosden's house.

We called Sully. I told her my theory about where the guns had come from, and it didn't involve Sarah Cosden. I had, in fact, seen a pair of dueling pistols just like them at Pete Morrison's studio. The pistols were among the many props he used in his historical paintings. I remembered them as soon as I saw the weapon Sully had carried out of Sarah's house. I was sure that if an analysis was done on the musket ball that had killed Rory, it would match the weapon we had found in Back Creek, not the pistol from Sarah's house.

Then there was the dress. When Sarah was found in Back Creek, she had been wearing a long calico dress—just the sort of thing that would have been in fashion a century ago. The dress could be explained away by the simple fact that it was hard to know the mental state of a distraught woman intent on committing suicide. She might have donned such a dress for reasons known only to her.

But there was another explanation. Sarah sometimes modeled for Pete Morrison, and she wore old-fashioned clothes when she did so. The dress, the antique pistols . . . they all pointed to the artist. But why? What connection did Pete Morrison have to the Cosden family?

Sully listened, but she wasn't happy about it.

"Please tell me what the hell you think you're doing? You're a renovator, not a detective."

"Then tell me why we're the ones who searched Back Creek, and not the police," I pointed out. "Mac and I—"

"You dragged Mac into this, huh? I shouldn't be surprised. You two are like a package deal. You're peanut butter, he's jelly. Or maybe bologna and cheese. Put him on."

I handed the phone to Mac and shot him a warning look. We were on skinny ice with the local police. From what I could see, what followed was a one-sided conversation, with Mac nodding as Sully bent his ear. He snapped shut the phone.

"What?" I looked at him expectantly.

"Three things," he said. "First, the county sheriff would be more than happy to accept that Sarah Cosden shot her cousin and then drowned herself. Case closed. But Sully convinced the sheriff to go out on a limb and request a search warrant for Pete Morrison's studio. Second, Sully relayed to me the fact that if we're wrong and we've made her beg the county sheriff to do this and it all amounts to nothing, then her ass is grass in the sheriff's office. Oh, and that she has a gun and won't hesitate to use it on us."

"That's so many things I've lost count. Was there anything else?"

"Actually, yes. The third thing is that Sully and I have a date tomorrow night."

"Well," I said, not entirely sure how I felt about that. But Mac had made it clear he wanted a crack at Sully. In accordance with the Code of Buddyhood, all I could do was force a smile. "That's something. Maybe you two can get something going."

"If she hasn't shot me first. She didn't sound real happy over the phone. And it depends on whether or not the deputies find anything at Pete Morrison's studio. They'll be heading

there in the next hour or two. Sully said that under no circumstances are we to be there."

Mac and I just grinned at that, then got back in the truck
and drove over to Pete's place.

We didn't have to wait long for the sheriff's deputies. I half
expected them to show up with lights and sirens, and maybe a
SWAT team in tow. This was murder we were talking about,
right? But there was just one vehicle, an unmarked county car,
and it obeyed the 20 mph speed limit on the road leading up to
Pete's house.

There was no need to hurry. Pete was nowhere in sight, and
his truck wasn't in the gravel driveway. Mac and I had been
sitting up the street from his cottage for half an hour, and there
hadn't been any sign of activity. Marsh Road dead-ended into
the grassy wetland that bordered the east end of town, so there
was only one way in or out. There were maybe a dozen modest
houses along the road, including Pete's. The houses were
spread out, well-separated by yards and gardens, so that Pete
had no immediate neighbors. His back yard overlooked the
marsh and canal in the distance. Out on the water, I could
make out the smokestack of a tug pushing a barge toward the
Chesapeake City bridge. The tug's engine growled as it strained
against the current.

Sully got out of the county car with the bald detective we
had seen her with at Sarah Cosden's house. We drove closer
and climbed out of the truck. Neither deputy looked all that
pleased to see us.

"What are you two doing here?" Sully snapped.

"We've taken things this far," I said. "We just want to see
what turns up at Pete's studio."

"You want me to arrest them?" her partner asked.

Sully seemed to take a moment to think about it. "That
won't be necessary, as long as they behave themselves. They *are*
the ones who managed to find the pistol in Back Creek, after

all. Boys, this is T.J., T.J., this is Mac and Tom."

"The ones with that home improvement show," he said. "I've checked it out online."

"Be sure to tell all your friends," I said.

"I'm glad that girl Jenny came back," T.J. remarked. He shot a grin at Mac. "She's pretty hot. I was getting tired of this one's big mug."

"Oh, I don't know," Sully said. "It kind of grows on you after a while."

Mac turned red as a Chesapeake Bay sunset at that remark.

"Better hang back," T.J. warned. "It doesn't look like Pete is home, but you never know when there's going to be trouble."

Pete might not have been there, but Picasso was home. The aging Labrador ambled out to bark at us, more in greeting than in warning. He lifted his head, tongue lolling, and let Mac scratch his ears. Then he tagged along at the deputies' heels as they went to knock on the front door. No answer.

"The warrant is strictly for the studio," T.J. explained. "Of course, if we happen to look in a window and see something in plain view, that's fair game."

The detective then proceeded to walk around Pete's cottage, peering in the windows. Picasso trailed him, panting from the effort. He must have been an old, old dog. Sully kept her eyes on Marsh Road, just in case Pete's truck came driving up.

T.J. continued on to the freestanding studio beside the cottage and again looked in the windows.

"No surprises this way," he explained. "Looks like nobody is home."

Nonetheless, as he reached for the door latch, the detective's other hand drifted to rest on the gun at his hip.

The door was not locked. That in itself wasn't entirely unusual—Chesapeake City was still that sort of town. There had been a murder, however, so people were being more careful. I couldn't help wondering who else but the murderer might feel comfortable still leaving the door open?

"Pete couldn't have gone far," Sully observed. "You don't

light out for Mexico and leave your doors unlocked. And you don't leave your dog behind."

"Seems to me he's got nothing to hide," T.J. said. He appeared to visibly relax. "As a general rule, people under suspicion tend to act suspiciously. I don't see much evidence of that, other than the fact that he doesn't happen to be home, and there's no law against that."

In other words, the deputies were starting to think that they had been sent on a wild goose chase—thanks in large part to me.

T.J. went in and I followed, ignoring Sully's shout of protest. "Hey—"

The studio looked much the same as I remembered it from my last visit. The canoe still took up most of the room, overflowing with props for Pete's historical paintings. Three or four paintings in various stages of completion stood waiting on their easels. One canvas showed the beginning stages of the painting I had commissioned of the Cosden House, to give as a gift to its owners. Pete had roughed in the canvas, if that was the term for it, sketching in the outline of the house and filling in some of the details with brush work. Curiously, the time period he had chosen was from when the house was new. On the street out front, he had painted in a horse and buggy. Cars had existed in 1913, but they would have been a novelty in a working town like Chesapeake City. Pete's painting was clearly a work in progress, because so far the painting lacked his characteristic detail. I knew for a fact that he would spend hours poring over old photographs or even visiting museums to get the details just right. Somehow, I doubted that was where he'd gone today.

Sully came in after me, followed closely by Picasso. With a contented groan, the old dog settled onto his cushion under the north-facing windows.

"You're not supposed to be in here," she said.

"Shouldn't you be watching the road?"

"I put Mac in charge of that. He used to be a cop, so I think he can handle it." She put her hands on her hips. "You, on the other hand, need to get out. We would be in so much hot water if the judge found out we let you in here."

"I'm the only one who's been in Pete's studio before," I said, determined not to budge an inch. "Besides, it seems to me that you're not looking for what's in here, but what's not."

"Then why don't you give us a clue," T.J. said.

"For starters, there's that painting right there." I nodded at another work in progress that showed a woman in a long, old-fashioned dress standing with a lantern and the town's light house in the background. Though in its early stages, the canvas showed a face that was unmistakably Sarah Cosden's.

"Well, that's interesting," T.J. said.

I looked around the room, filled with old saddles, swords, vintage hats, and even piles of horseshoes. If the artist thing didn't work out, Pete could open an antiques shop, or maybe supply props for movie production companies. While the studio overflowed with items, what I didn't see may have been the most interesting objects of all.

"I don't see those dueling pistols anywhere," I said. "The last time I was here, they were in plain sight."

"Look at this place," Sully said, gazing around at the clutter. "How could you possibly tell what's here and what's not?"

"The dueling pistols aren't here," I insisted. "They were absolutely the same weapons you took out of Sarah Cosden's house and that Mac and I found in Back Creek."

"The question is, how did they get in those places?"

"I'm afraid that to get your answer, you're going to have to find Pete Morrison."

At the mention of his master's name, Picasso thumped his tail. The old dog wouldn't be the only one who was happy to see Pete, who had some explaining to do.

CHAPTER 21

The next morning, I got up extra early, putting aside all thoughts of dueling pistols, suicide, murder and Sears houses at the bottom of Chesapeake Bay. Pete was still nowhere to be found, so all those questions surrounding him would have to wait. Besides, I told myself as I swung by a convenience store to pick up a large coffee, black, and a couple doughnuts, Sully was right when she said this was a police matter. I was happy to let her and the other deputies catch the killer. I had an old house to renovate.

A renovation that was behind schedule, I reminded myself. Now that I thought about it, I couldn't remember a time when we had ever been *ahead* of schedule, or even *right on* schedule. What renovation project is ever anything but running late?

"It's about time you showed up," Jenny said when she saw me hurry through the front door of the Cosden House. She was busy rehanging a closet door.

I glanced at my watch. It wasn't even seven, so I was surprised to find anyone else there. I regretted my snappy comeback as soon as the words left my mouth: "Some of us haven't had a week-long vacation." I knew Jenny was just joshing me about being late, but for some reason her words felt like vinegar splashed on an open wound. Jenny had that effect on me lately. She could just as easily have said "Good morning" and it would have gone on like oil-base paint over latex. Deep down, I knew I wasn't mad at Jenny at all but at myself for jumping into bed with her in the first place. I was the boss; I should have known better. But I'd gone ahead and done it anyway. There was no accounting for love—or lust, to be more accurate.

"I could take a permanent vacation, if you'd like." Her tone this time was not playful and the way that Jenny was holding the hammer in her hand, I was half afraid that she was going to use it on me.

I took a deep breath. "Can I get a do over? It's going to be a long day if this is how we start our morning."

Jenny grunted something unintelligible as she attacked a hinge pin.

I turned around and made my entrance again. "Good morning," I said, forcing myself to smile. "Sleep well?"

"What kind of a question is that?" She smacked the pin home. "Do you really think I slept well if I'm here so early? And if I didn't sleep, dammit, it's mainly because of you."

"Let's try this again." I retreated to the front porch, paused long enough to take a sip of coffee, and went in again. Jenny was waiting for me with her hammer and an expression that could best be described as glowering.

"One word and you're going to get a claw hammer between the eyes."

Point taken, I swept past her into the kitchen, our *de facto* base of operations. There, I drank more coffee and went over our list of projects for the day. When renovating an old house—and especially when doing so for our sometimes chaotic *Delmarva Renovators* where so much coordination was involved—it paid to be organized. It was a little like being a general fighting a battle in that you had to stick with your battle plan and not allow yourself to be distracted by all the skirmishes. I suppose I was more like General Chaos than General Patton when it came to directing the troops. Our punch list for today included fixing squeaky stair treads (the repairing of which was to be filmed for a segment on our site), installing the upstairs bathroom fixtures (also to be filmed), taping and mudding a closet that Mac had added to one of the bedrooms, and finally doing something about that god-awful gaping hole in the dining room left when we had moved the basement steps. The hole was covered in plywood, but somehow I thought the homeowners might want something more permanent.

I spent about twenty minutes in the kitchen, sipping my coffee and listening to Jenny wield her hammer with particular vigor. Finally, out back, I heard our work van pull up. Time to get cracking. Happily, I realized I hadn't thought about the Cosdens once since I'd walked in the door of their old house this morning.

In accordance with my battle plan, we attacked the squeaky stair treads first. This was hardly a major structural issue, or even a minor one, but that squeak whenever we stepped on the third and fifth steps was annoying. Kind of the old house version of a hang nail. The Pritchards surely wouldn't want to put up with it. And while the stairs were in no danger of collapsing, that recurring squeak—or maybe it was more properly described as a creak—did not create a good impression regarding the overall structural integrity of the Cosden House. Fortunately, it was easy enough to fix and the repair would make for good video. It was dark in the closet under the stairs, so Kat and Iggy set up lights for filming our repairs.

Jenny got going, sounding so energetic and upbeat that you'd hardly have known she was ready to hit me with a hammer half an hour ago: "It's our good luck that we can access the underside of the staircase. If your stairs are enclosed, your job is much more difficult. Today, we are going to use two simple items to eliminate the squeak that's developed over ninety-plus years."

Jenny went on to explain that most creaky steps were caused by the wooden joints or edges rubbing together. Over time, wood shrinks and gaps form. Sometimes, a dry lubricant such as graphite might temporarily take care of the squeak, but the best fix was to do away with these gaps. On camera, Jenny gently tapped thin wooden wedges into the gap that had appeared between the tread (the horizontal or "step" part of the stair) and the riser (the vertical section). Then, for good measure, Jenny used short screws to install metal shelf brackets on the underside of the stairs. She had come up with that one herself, and I thought it was pretty clever.

"What we are doing is helping to redistribute the weight of someone on the step while at the same time forming a more solid bond between riser and tread," she explained.

The day went quickly after that as we moved from the stairs to the plumbing fixtures—washers, Teflon tape, caulk—to a dozen other small tasks, going down the list I'd written in the kitchen. By lunchtime, we had progressed to taping and applying mud (never a carpenter's favorite job) and by the time late afternoon rolled around we were contemplating the gaping hole in the dining room floor. The rectangular hole measured four feet by eight feet where the basement steps had once been located. The wall and the door to the steps had since been removed to make the room bigger.

"This is going to be a challenge," Jenny said, surveying the job. She seemed to be in a better mood, even though we were alone together. "What's your plan, Stan?"

"We could put down plywood and carpet the floor, but it wouldn't match the rest of the downstairs," I said. All the other rooms had their original hardwood floors, which would be sanded and refinished as the house neared completion. "Plus it's not what the homeowners want."

"The easy way never is," Jenny agreed. She studied the floor and announced: "Patch job."

"Easier said than done." First, we had to sister new two-by-ten floor joists into place to span the gap and provide support for the floor, plus give us something to nail into. That kind of heavy construction was Mac's provenance. Jen would finesse the floor, which required the sort of patience that would soon have had Mac throwing things, like maybe the miter saw. The "patch job" as Jenny called it, required some creative scrounging. One simply couldn't go to the nearest home center for new tongue-and-groove floorboards circa 1913—and the local sawmill that produced the floorboards had long since closed. So I had scavenged floorboards where I could—some taken up from the attic floor, which would be used for storage anyhow, so a perfect floor wasn't needed up there. A few shorter boards came from the flooring inside the bedroom closets. These salvaged boards were now stacked to one side, covered with a canvas drop cloth so that we didn't accidentally grab them for any other purpose.

"Tomorrow," Jenny said.

I glanced at my watch—a Timex my boys had given me for Father's Day—and was surprised to discover that it was already after six o'clock. Some renovating days were like that. The good ones. If our crew got in a few more days like this one, we could complete the Cosden House by our Canal Day deadline. Now that the end was finally in sight, I felt a sense of relief mixed with regret. Just a few days ago, I had despaired of ever completing the project. But the thought that we might actually finish and move on made me realize how much I would miss the old place. It felt like an old friend. I was also worried because we had nothing else lined up. Nothing definite, at least. Our online show was catching on, but not to the point where our phone was ringing off the hook with projects or my email inbox was overflowing with invitations to repair someone's old house.

Mac bounded through the door, making the windows rattle. "Quittin' time for me, Hammer," he boomed. "I've got a hot date."

I was so surprised you could have pushed me over with a paint-stirring stick. But then I remembered that Mac had mentioned it yesterday. We had been so busy that I had forgotten all about it. "Right," I said. "With Sully."

Mac grinned. "We're going to an indoor shooting range over in Delaware," he said. "Loser buys dinner."

"I wish you had reminded me. You're knocking off kind of early," I said, sounding more put out than I intended. Mac didn't notice. I glanced at Jenny—who was looking at me, noticing my reaction. She'd heard that note of—of *what*, I asked myself, *jealousy?*—in my voice.

"What are you, my mother?" Mac asked good-naturedly. "Anyhow, we were so busy today that I just forgot all about it."

Not likely. "Have a good time," I said, struggling to sound enthusiastic. "You want the truck? I can ride back in the van."

"Sully is going to pick me up," he said. "I'll shower at her place."

I was more than a little taken aback. What was next? Sleeping over? Should I remind him to bring his toothbrush? "Have a good time," I said, a bit weakly. Then, trying harder: "Try not to shoot anybody at the gun range."

"Don't wait up for me." Mac winked and then lumbered through the door to wait on the front porch for his ride.

Jenny was still watching me. When we were alone, she said in mock surprise, "Why, Tom. If I didn't know better I'd say you were jealous."

The thought occurred to me that the woman I had recently slept with might not appreciate that sentiment on my part toward another woman. "No," I hurried to say. "Of course not. I'm just worried that Mac is going to get . . . distracted."

"Is that what they're calling it these days?" She turned to go. "You're the boss, Tom, but just remember that you can't control everything."

Soon after, Mac left with Sully, and an hour later the rest of our crew packed up and headed back to the hotel. Jenny and Kat were planning an impromptu girls night out. Pizza and a chick flick. They asked me along, but I begged off, knowing that I'd be as welcome as a bent nail.

"I have some things I want to finish up here," I said.

So I hung around the Cosden House, sweeping up, taking stock, and thinking in the quiet that the empty house afforded. Jenny had accused me of being jealous of Mac, and I was trying to wrap my head around that. Was she right?

Mac and I had leaned on each other through some tough times. Mac's failed business. My painful separation from my wife. We had each other's back. That's what buddies did. I thought about him and Sully. Mac hadn't had a girlfriend in some time. Part of the reason, I suspected, was that bankruptcy is not a powerful aphrodisiac at an age when women are looking for security. In the last few months, our mutual attitude might have been expressed as, "Women, who needs 'em!" It was a convenient lie we told ourselves to get through the hard times. And now Sully had come along and popped the soap bubble we had blown for ourselves and crawled into.

I took out a load of scrap lumber, enjoying the fresh air of the spring evening. On going back in, I recognized that unique smell that the Cosden House had. Old houses had distinct aromas, almost like wines. True, some smelled musty and damp, but that faded with a good airing out. An old house needed fresh air like everything else. Individual woods, horsehair plaster, varnishes and paints, wallpapers and carpets all gave off their smells, tinged with dankness or dustiness. Maybe you caught a whiff of a long-ago uncle's cherry pipe tobacco. Then there were a few thousand meals cooked in the days when people really knew their way around a kitchen. Roasts, Thanksgiving dinners, fresh-baked bread, coffee. Wine connoisseurs tried to impress you with descriptions of a cabernet with aromas of blackberries and chocolate or by describing a bordeaux as having a "good nose," but could they unravel or even begin to describe the intricate smells of an old house?

I went upstairs, noting with satisfaction that the steps did not creak. Our small repair earlier in the day had given the old house a new solidity. Iggy would edit the video into a three-minute segment and post it on our site. Earlier on in the short history of worthsaving.com, I had tried to do everything my-self, from shooting the videos to hosting to managing our website. If you had looked up the definition of "Jack-of-all-trades and master-of-none" you would have seen my name. I soon found that Jenny was a better host—make that hostess—with far more screen appeal and that Iggy was an editing genius who could handle video better and faster than I ever could. If one walked past his hotel room door late at night, you could hear music—usually classic punk, if that wasn't an oxy-moron—as he stayed up until all hours working on video. That left me to do all the blogging, which was fine with me, since words always had been more of my forte than the visual end of things. This division of labor was no different from how cer-tain carpenters had specialties. Some did framing, some finish work, and there were those who only built stairs. I supposed that I was a carpenter who specialized in building blogs.

There was still plenty of work to be done on the second floor. In the master bedroom, the large windows that over-looked the canal still needed trim. Where the ceiling fan should be located there was just a tangle of wires. This would be the only room in the house with wall-to-wall carpet, but so far the bedroom still had bare floorboards. The result was a hollow space in which every noised echoed. All in all the remaining work didn't seem like much, until you considered that in most house projects the last ten percent of work ended up taking about ninety percent of the time. The devil—and the labor—was in the details.

As I took a mental inventory of the room, from somewhere deep inside the Cosden House I half heard a creak and pop, followed by another. Footsteps? No, everyone else had gone home. Then came the distinct whine of a cordless drill. That was weird. It must have come from a neighbor's house. On a street filled with historical homes, we weren't the only ones with an old house project going on.

I crossed the hallway to the bath, noting how dim and shadowy it had become at the other end of the hall, near the doors to the remaining bedrooms and the attic. I went into the bath and took stock. There was a lot more to be done here, too. The vanity was in place, but not the sink fixtures. The tile work was finished, but the walls needed another coat of paint. The lights had not been wired in yet, so that the bath was dim and dusky.

Downstairs, I heard the steady creaking of what I was now certain must be footsteps. Furtive ones. It was possible that someone had wandered in off the street to poke around. Brazen as that seemed, it had already happened more than once. People in town seemed to feel that our old house project was as much theirs as ours, given the Cosden House's place in local history.

"Hello?" I called.

There was no answer, but the creaking noise stopped. I hadn't been worried before, but now a sense of uneasiness crept over me. I was pretty sure that someone was downstairs. So many strange things had happened in the house, and I had to be honest that like everyone else in town, between Rory's death and then Sarah's suicide, you might say that I was a little edgy. I looked around for some kind of weapon, then chastised myself for being paranoid.

Nor was I about to hide upstairs. I started down the steps, my feet silent on our newly repaired treads. I caught myself trying to be stealthy, like someone in a horror movie, until I remembered that I was the one who was supposed to be here.

"Hello?" I called again. "Jen? Is that you?"

Still no answer. I moved forward into the foyer. The shadows had lengthened considerably until dusk spilled into all the corners. Not so much as a car passed in the street. It could have been 1913 all over again.

Some flicker of motion caught my eye. My heart made like a Porsche, going from zero to sixty in about six seconds. I could hear my heartbeat thundering in my ears. Moving across the foyer, I groped for a light switch. The sudden light revealed Pete Morrison standing there.

In a way, I wasn't all that surprised to see him. I had helped the police look for him just yesterday, so maybe he had come looking for me this time around. That, and the fact that the Cosden House seemed to be Ground Zero for trouble in Chesapeake City. So no, I wasn't all that surprised to see Pete. What threw me for a loop was the oversized grilling fork in his hand.

"Pete," I said. And then the obvious question: "What are you doing here?"

"I was looking for you."

I nodded at the large, two-pronged fork he held. "I don't suppose you came to invite me to a cookout?"

Pete smiled in a way that made beads of sweat break out on my forehead. "Something like that, actually."

That's when I decided to take a closer look at the barbecue fork he held. It was maybe a foot-and-a-half long. However, my relief that he wasn't wielding a knife or a gun quickly dissipated. An orange extension cord snaked around the handle. Pete had cut off the plug and split the insulated coating to reveal bare copper wires that reflected the dim light like snake's eyes. These wires were twisted around the prongs and secured with black electrical tape. In my mind's eye I could almost see the sparking current running through those tines. The fork's wooden handle insulated Pete from the electrical charge, but if he stuck that fork in anyone, they'd be done. Like me, for instance. He was planning a cookout, all right.

"Pete, let's talk about this," I said.

"Don't bother running," he said, taking a step toward me. "I screwed the doors and windows shut so you can't get out."

That explained the drill I'd heard. "This is insane!"

"I've never tried this before, but I'm thinking it will look like a heart attack," he said with a chillingly matter-of-fact tone. "I couldn't just shoot you, you see. That would cause too much trouble right now."

"Gosh, the last thing I'd want to cause you is trouble," I said sarcastically. Now I was getting mad. But I forced myself to take a deep breath. Anger would likely get me killed. Pete had planned this out. What I had to do was outsmart him. But it was a little tough to do with him waving the Electric Fork of Death at me.

I retreated another step, and Pete advanced. I could see that he had electrified the fork with one of our longest extension cords. He could follow me anywhere in the house. I started to feel like a mouse in a snake cage.

"I thought about breaking your neck and making it look like you fell off a ladder," he said. "But I didn't feel like wrestling you. Frankly, I wasn't sure that I'd win. I've got a few years on you, you know."

"Pete—"

"I would have let you alone," he said, moving closer. I expected him to look wild-eyed and crazed, but his demeanor was frighteningly calm. "None of this was your quarrel. It had to do with us Cosdens. But you had to go play detective and sic the police on me. That's meddling in affairs that don't concern you, Tom. You'll only cause more trouble for me. I am sorry, though. I do like you."

It was small comfort that the man who was about to skewer me with an electrified grilling fork found me agreeable company. Something else Pete said got my attention. "What do you mean by 'us Cosdens'? You're not even from around here."

"No, I'm not. But I am a Cosden, just as much as Captain Ezra or Sarah or Rory. You see, Leo Cosden was my grandfather."

"The body in the wall," I said.

"That's right. I never had any real proof of what Ezra had done until you found my grandfather's body. There was the evidence that he murdered my grandfather—his own brother. I already knew how Captain Ezra Cosden had turned away my grandmother when she showed up in Chesapeake City, pregnant with Leo's baby. They were going to get married, you know, until he was lost in the storm. That house on board was for her. But Ezra and the rest of the Cosdens turned her away.

You can imagine what it was like for an unwed mother in those days. My mother was born into a life of poverty, always moving from one hovel to the next. She died young, like her own mother before her. They knew what the Cosdens had done to them. I knew. And I decided a long time ago that I would make them pay."

"So you killed them."

"They were trying to keep you from discovering the truth," Pete said. "If this had turned out differently, Tom, you could have thanked me. Thanked me for protecting you. Why do you think Rory got involved in the first place, helping out around the house? He wanted to keep an eye on things. And then, when you got too close to the truth, he turned on you."

"But Sarah? What harm could she possibly have done?"

"She pushed Iver Jones down the stairs for helping you. How's that for harmless. You and your crew might have been next."

"So you took matters into your own hands."

"Sarah was the hard one to kill," he said. "She was modeling for me, so I had her meet me at the harbor that morning. She never suspected a thing. I brought her a cup of coffee that I'd drugged with a leftover prescription. Then I held her head under water."

I felt sick to my stomach. "And Rory?"

"I drove out to his trailer and ordered him into his truck at gunpoint. Then I shot him and staged the accident in Back Creek."

"You planted the bill of sale for the Sears house."

"Yes. Rory wasn't the only one who went through the Cosden papers at the historical society. I put the bill of sale in Rory's trailer, after I killed him. It seemed like the best way to let everyone know what Rory was hiding. To show his guilt."

"So Sarah pushed Iver. Rory slashed our tires." I edged away, trying to buy time. "Who threw the brick through our window?"

Pete blinked and gave me a blank look. "What brick?"

"Never mind."

He waved the fork. "I'm thinking your neck would be good," he said. "Nice, bare flesh. The current should go right in."

I wasn't planning on standing still for that. If Pete was dragging an extension cord, I knew I could outrun him. So I turned and ran. The front door was, indeed, screwed shut. Pete had driven a couple of drywall screws at an angle through the door and into the frame. Under different circumstances, I might even have been impressed by his carpentry skills.

"See?" he said, following me in no particular hurry. "I wasn't kidding. The back door is the same. If you stand still, Tom, I'll make it quick for you. But if you make me chase you around the house, well, I won't make any promises."

"You're insane."

"Me? You're the one who's being irrational, Tom. Accept your fate, all one hundred and twenty volts of it."

I had no doubt now that Pete had secured the back door as well. And the windows. Briefly, I considered what kind of weapon I could use against Pete. It just figured that there wasn't so much as a hammer lying around—the only tool in sight was a tape measure, and what was I going to do with that, threaten to measure him for a coffin? My only real defense was that I knew the Cosden House better than he did.

I dashed into the dining room, where we had left the plywood off the hole in the floor where the cellar stairs used to be. Pete was still in the next room, but I could hear him dragging the extension cord. It made a slithering sound, like a snake. Quickly, I grabbed the canvas drop cloth covering the stack of spare floorboards and whipped it across the hole, like a waiter snaps out a fresh tablecloth. It looked like we had spread it there to protect the floor from paint splatters. Not much of a trap, so I prayed that Pete wasn't paying attention to where he was stepping.

Pete came in. I was cornered now with no way out.

"Your friends aren't here to help you now," he said. "Not

Mac, and not Deputy Sullivan. Good-looking girl, Sully."

"You wouldn't have stopped with Sarah and Rory," I said, trying to keep him talking and distracted. "Who was next?"

"Edith is next," he admitted. He smiled. "After *you*, of course. That old lady knew the truth about what her father had done to our branch of the Cosdens. She's as bad as all the rest. But I'm in no hurry about her. And no one will suspect a thing. Old ladies have accidents all the time."

He was almost to the canvas drop cloth. I backed away and Pete came closer. One more step. I shrank against the wall, trying to looked trapped, which wasn't very hard under the circumstances. Up until now, Pete had been so calm and deliberate, but I had to make sure he moved too fast to regain his balance if he started to fall.

"One more thing before you kill me," I said. "There's no point in telling anything now but the truth. I always thought you were a lousy artist. What's the word I'm looking for in describing your work? Derivative. And let's not forget hokey and commercial. I mean, how many pictures of sailboats and sunsets can a guy paint before he starts to retch?"

That stopped Pete in his tracks, which wasn't quite the effect I'd intended. "I wasn't going to before, but I think I can say now that I'm going to enjoy this," he snarled. Then Pete rushed forward to skewer me. He stepped onto the drop cloth. Miraculously, the canvas seemed to support him for the space of a heartbeat, the fabric taut as a drum. And then the drop cloth gave way, pitching Pete into the dark cellar below.

CHAPTER 22

Canal Day dawned bright, sunny and so humid you could have wrung out the air like a wet beach towel. That didn't stop the cars from pouring into town. Boy Scouts waved the arriving traffic toward parking spaces in the fields at the edge of town because the little village literally couldn't hold that many vehicles. A shuttle bus brought people from the parking areas.

"Always one of the hottest days of the year," remarked Carl Batzer, who was busy keeping the coffee flowing in his crowded café, but not too busy to chat a while. His café was filled with hungry boaters who had moored in the harbor for the festival. The official event lasted just one day, but there was no telling that to the boaters, who began claiming mooring space two or even three nights before Canal Day. Carl was happy to see them. He'd even come up with a special menu to streamline things. The special was something called a "Crab Raft," which was basically an omelet topped with a scoop of crab meat, for the steep price of nine dollars. The locals thought that was highway robbery for an omelet, but the boaters all seemed to want one, much to Carl's delight.

"Crowded," Mac grumped beside me.

"I'll make more this weekend than I would in two weeks normally," Carl confided to us, lowering his voice. "Canal Day puts me in the black for the year. I sure am glad the rain stopped."

Yesterday's weather had been cause for concern. In a tourist town, I was learning that the weather on a holiday weekend or special event could make or break a small business. After a dry spring, the rain came down all at once. Buckets of it, soaking into the ground, spilling over the gutters, puddling in the streets so that small cars were almost up to their hubcaps.

"Into every life a little rain must fall," Mac had remarked, two cups of coffee in hand, as we stood on the front porch of the Cosden House and watched the deluge.

It was a platitude, and yet recent events had added weight to his words. Rain had fallen, and so had Pete Morrison. Fallen hard. I didn't feel sorry about that. The tumble into the cellar had left the artist with two broken legs and a fractured skull. That had been two weeks ago. He was still in Cecil County General Hospital. It was unlikely that he might escape, but Sully had seen to it that one wrist was handcuffed to the hospital bed. Pete had confessed to killing two people, after all, and murder was rare enough on this part of the Eastern Shore that the police weren't taking any chances.

On the porch, Mac had handed me a mug of coffee. I took a sip and detected the sharp bite of bourbon. "It's not five o'clock," I said in mock indignation. "Doesn't that make bourbon in one's coffee indecent?"

"Nah," Mac said, taking a deep sip and smacking his lips. "After what we've been through, Hammer, I'd say we deserve this shot."

I thought about that, taking stock. Two murders. An attack by a killer wielding an electrified barbecue fork. The scramble to finish an old house project on deadline. "Come to think of it, maybe we deserve two shots of that bourbon."

Mac laughed. "I wouldn't argue."

But neither of us made a move to get out of our rocking chairs to fetch the bottle. It was an errand that required too much energy. The last few days had been exhausting as we rushed to finish the house in time for Canal Day, much less keep our website updated. We had managed to knock out those final items on our punch list. Ceiling fans were hung in the bedroom. Window and door trim was in place. The upstairs bathroom had a second coat of paint. Just about everything that needed to be was nailed down, caulked, or painted. Just in time for the owners' Canal Day housewarming party.

We'd been at the house since early that morning, making a few final touches and watching the Canal Day preparations. Mac and I walked down to get some breakfast at the café. Wearing blaze orange safety vests, volunteers from the Lions Club were setting up barricades to close off the street to vehicles. Today, Canal Town's old streets would be reserved for pedestrians.

The timing of the rain had been perfect, giving the town a just-washed feel. Everything looked fresh, right down to the colorful wood siding of the old houses and the electric blue hydrangea blossoms in the gardens and the petunias in hanging baskets on front porches. It seemed impossible that this same town had been stricken with murder and mayhem just a few days before. But that was the thing about quaint old towns. Some might call it a façade, a face the town put on for tourists, but I believed it went deeper than that. Old towns and old houses possessed a spirit that ran deep and reached back centuries in some cases. It took more than the occasional madman and murderer to leave a lasting impression. If you've seen how seemingly powerful waves bear down on a seawall and then disappear in a fury of foam and noise, you have a pretty good idea of what I mean.

Matt and I ordered and ate quickly because the café was too crowded to talk.

"More coffee?" Carl waved his steaming pot at me and Mac. I glanced over my shoulder at the line of people waiting to get in.

"No thanks. I've got somebody to see," I said. Carl's eyes flicked to the door, and I could see the eagerness on his face to make room for a couple of new diners—maybe ones who'd want to order up that nine-dollar Crab Float omelet. Mac and I slid off our stools. "Hot seats this morning."

I started to put a bill on the counter, but Carl waved me off. "You guys are regulars. At least you have been since you've been in town. It's on the house for putting up with the crowd this morning."

"You really don't—"

"I can afford to be generous today," Carl said. "Besides, the least I can do is give breakfast to the guy who ended the killings."

As we slipped out the crowded doorway, Mac said, "Rumor has it that Carl hasn't given anything away since Ronald Reagan was president. That includes gift certificates for the Little League fundraiser. You must have made an impression. So tell me, who's this person you've got to see?"

"Top secret," I replied, for no other reason than I knew it would drive Mac nuts. It was too much fun for me to resist pushing Mac's buttons once in a while. And truth be told, I was still feeling peevish about his new relationship with Sully. It was hard to get my head around them as, well, a couple. So I took revenge where I could, even if I realized it was petty and childish. "I'll see you later at the party."

"You'll tell me then?"

"Of course I will."

Now that the streets had been closed to vehicles, they were filling up with festival-goers. Crafters and vendors had set up tables on both sides of the streets, usually under a tarp to keep the sun off. The vendors were vetted and first preference was given to those who made and sold their own goods, rather than a bunch of junk from China. I passed a woodcarver offering beautifully grained bowls hand-made on a lathe, a potter who created vases and yet more bowls from local clay, more kitschy offerings such as "Welcome to the Beach" signs hand-painted on driftwood. Yet someone else was selling lawn ornaments they had cast in concrete: lions, gargoyles, gnomes with creepy, unseeing eyes. Next door to the stone animals, some poor sunburned author was flogging copies of his Civil War novel. There were local artists too numerous to count, and with a pang I thought of the boxes of prints Pete had ordered just for this day. Now, I supposed that no one would ever see his Chesapeake City scenes, which was a shame, considering that he really was a good artist. Maybe it had been a low blow to call him a hack that day at the Cosden House, but he had been trying to kill me at the time, after all. Under the circumstances, hurling an insult seemed permissible.

Down at the waterfront, various vendors were selling food. The smell of all those grills was delicious, and underneath it all was the tangy scent of lemonade. Non-profit groups like the Boy Scouts and Lions Club ran most of the stands, and their sales of burgers, barbecue chicken, sausages, crab cakes, and cold sodas and beer kept them funded through the year.

Out on the harbor, all sorts of hijinks were taking place, from water balloon fights to heavy drinking. It was a party on the water, with lots of bare flesh and bikinis. It was enough of a show that a crowd had developed on the dock just to watch.

I didn't join the spectators, however. My destination was historic Franklin Hall that loomed over the waterfront. Iver Jones was keeping the town historical society open for visitors, although from what I had seen out on the harbor, I doubted that most of the Canal Day crowd had history on their minds.

Eagerly awaiting his first visitors, reading glasses propped on his nose, Iver sat behind a desk strewn with newspaper clippings and town artifacts such as bottles from the A.E. Sprague soda plant. "I thought you'd be up at the Cosden House for the housewarming party," he said.

"That's later. You're going, aren't you?"

"The new owners *finally* got around to inviting me."

"Of course they did," I said. "You're the town historian, not to mention the resident expert on the Cosden House. Which is what I wanted to ask you about."

"Oh?"

"Come now, Iver," I said, realizing that I sounded like a

character in an English novel, so I tried for Raymond Chandler instead. "Don't play dumb with me. I think you know a lot more about the Cosden House than you ever let on."

"I don't know what you're talking about."

"You know what gets me? The biggest clue we had was when someone tossed a brick through the window with Leo Cosden's name scratched into it."

"Can't get much more obvious than that," Iver agreed.

"The funny thing is, Pete Morrison didn't throw that brick. He just gave me a blank look when I mentioned it."

"You'd believe a murderer?"

"In this case, I do. And I know that Rory and Sarah didn't throw that brick. They didn't want anyone to know it was their Great Uncle Leo who had tumbled out of that wall. No, it was someone who suspected the truth about how Leo's body came to be in the house. Someone who knew some of the Cosdens's dirty little secrets, but didn't want to get involved directly. This person had to go on living in town, when all was said and done. Maybe this person figured it would be better to let some newcomer such as myself meddle in things. I smiled. "You know what I think, Iver? I think you've got a pretty good arm."

We sat there for a moment in silence, like two chess players studying their pieces. The thick walls of Franklin Hall insulated us from the noise of the Canal Day crowd outside. Then a family wandered in, blinking at the transition from bright sunshine to the interior gloom. "Is this the museum?" the father asked.

Iver rose to greet them, then turned to me. He had taken something wrapped in plain brown paper from the floor beside his chair. "Would you make sure the new owners get this? Don't say that it's from me, just that it's a housewarming present," he said. "See you at the party."

The Canal Day crowds were even thicker now, and it took me a while to make my way the three blocks to the Cosden House, where the housewarming party had already begun. Jenny was on the front porch, in a pair of short-shorts and one of the Delmarva Renovators golf shirts I'd ordered for the occasion. She looked better in hers than I looked in mine. How in the world did she manage to look so sexy all the time? Considering that I had sworn her off, it almost wasn't fair, like waving chocolate bars in front of someone on a diet.

She raised a cocktail glass filled with lemonade and ice. "To our first project," she said.

I fished around in an ice-filled tub and came up with a chilled bottle of water. "To *Delmarva Renovators*," I agreed.

"You did a good job, Tom," she said. "You really pulled it off."

"We all did."

I went inside. Kat was in the foyer, wearing a flowery cocktail dress. I was taken aback.

"Look at you," I said.

Kat blushed. "I get tired of wearing the same old thing, you know. Jen helped me pick it out."

"Well, you look very nice."

Marsha was in the living room, explaining to someone about the drapery fabric. Out the window, I glimpsed Iggy in the side yard, smoking a cigarette.

For the most part, the party had ended up where parties always do, in the kitchen. Mac was there, hovering over a platter of hors d'oeuvres with a cold beer in one hand. Sully was next to him, looking good in her off-duty shorts and T-shirt. Those two had been spending a lot of time together. Mac caught my eye and winked.

The Pritchards were holding court, sharing anecdotes about the house and accepting compliments from their friends. And why shouldn't they? I could see that Mac was listening with a barely contained smirk on his face, but it was their money that had fixed up the house, and they had put their share of sweat and hard work into the house as well. You could even say that they had truly earned this house. And the project had turned out well enough that it looked like we would be getting another old house lined up for *Delmarva Renovators*. Our show was still a go, at least for now.

The Pritchards introduced me around to their friends and relatives, who seemed nice enough. Their guests *oohed* and *aahed* at the renovated house, walking from room to room. For some reason I felt nervous, as if I were undergoing some sort of final exam. Is an old house ever really done? In the eyes of the renovator, there's always some glaring flaw or a repair that didn't quite seem to turn out. And given time—a week, a month, a year—something would have to be fixed all over again. The plumbing might spring a leak, a door might start to stick. It was the nature of old houses that they were works in progress. But for now, today, I suppose I should consider the project done.

Jenny came in from the front porch, and from the other end of the house she caught my eye and mouthed a single word: "Relax."

I noticed that the patch in the dining room floor was done so well that you would hardly know a small-town murderer had nearly fallen to his own death there. Old houses have secrets—here was another.

I was still carrying the package Iver had given me, so I returned to the kitchen and presented it to Cindy Pritchard. I had meant for Pete to paint her something that featured the house, but that canvas was still in his studio, unfinished. Cindy unwrapped the brown paper and pronounced it perfect, although I could tell she was a little puzzled.

"I can see it's Chesapeake City," she said. "But who are those boys?"

Who knew where Iver had found it, but he had come across a sepia-toned photograph in an old-fashioned frame of two boys, both about twelve, in their Sunday best. They stood at the waterfront, with the masts and rigging of ships in the background. It was still an era when people were trained not to smile in photographs. But neither did they frown. An impish light shined in the boys' eyes. They bore an unmistakable resemblance to one another. Brothers. Iver had said that the two had been inseparable as boys, like the Tom Sawyer and Huck Finn of Chesapeake City. Before they were rivals. Someone had salvaged this photograph and saved it down through the years. And why not? Wouldn't we all prefer to remember the better times, the happier memories.

"Leo and Ezra Cosden," I explained.

Cindy took down another picture, and in its place I hung the frame so that now the Cosden brothers stood side by side, keeping an eye on the old house that was as much theirs as ours.

About the Author

David Healey is the author of several novels and nonfiction books, including *Sharpshooter* and *1812: Rediscovering Chesapeake Bay's Forgotten War*. A graduate of Washington College and the Stonecoast MFA program, he enjoys working around his old house and has been known to drive his family crazy by making frequent stops to read historical markers at the side of the road.

www.davidhealey.net

CPSIA information can be obtained at www.ICGtesting.com
Printed in the USA
LVOW130737230613

339671LV00001B/27/P